A
LITTLE
IN LOVE

A LITTLE IN LOVE

SUSAN E. FLETCHER

Chicken House

SCHOLASTIC INC. | NEW YORK

Based on the original classic novel by Victor Hugo

Text copyright © 2015 by Susan E. Fletcher

First published in the United Kingdom in 2014 by Chicken House, 2 Palmer
Street, Frome, Somerset BA11 1DS.

Library of Congress Cataloging-in-Publication Data

Fletcher, Susan E., 1979– author.
    A little in love / Susan E. Fletcher.—First edition.
        pages cm
    "Based on the original classic novel by Victor Hugo."
Summary: Eponine, the street girl from Les Misérables, tells the story of her life
and her unrequited love for Marius, which ultimately leads to her death on the
barricades during the short-lived rebellion of June 1832.
    ISBN 978-0-545-82960-1
1. Hugo, Victor, 1802–885. Misérables—Adaptations. 2. Riots—France—
Paris—Juvenile fiction. 3. Man-woman relationships—Juvenile fiction.
4. Paris (France)—History—19th century—Juvenile fiction. 5. France—
History—Louis Philippe, 1830–1848—Juvenile fiction. [1. Love—Fiction.
2. Riots—Fiction. 3. Paris (France)—History—19th century—Fiction.
4. France—History—Louis Philippe, 1830–1848—Fiction.] I. Title.
    PZ7.1.F58Li 2015
    823.92—dc23
    [Fic]

2015001439

10 9 8 7 6 5 4 3 2 1   15 16 17 18 19

Printed in the U.S.A.   23
First edition, September 2015
Book design by Yaffa Jaskoll

*"Et puis, tenez, Monsieur Marius, je crois que
j'étais un peu amoureuse de vous."*

"You know, Monsieur Marius, I think I was a
little in love with you."

VICTOR HUGO, *LES MISÉRABLES*

RUE DE LA CHANVRERIE,
5 JUNE 1832

I'm dying. There's no use hoping I'll live or telling myself, *Keep going, it's only a small wound.* There's too much blood on the ground.

I'm going to die in this street.

I can hardly breathe. My hand, my arm, and my body are so full of pain. I'm whimpering, trembling. And I'm cold too—lying on my back with the cobblestones pressing into me. In the distance are horses' hooves, and someone is shouting, "Is anyone alive out there?" I want to call, *"Yes, over here!"* But I can't. It hurts too much to speak or move.

I can smell gunpowder. And burning wood. The barricade's still alight, filling the air with thick black smoke. It protected us for a while, this wall, but not now. The soldiers broke through it, set it on fire with their musket shots. It's crackling near me, turning to ash, and like all the people who are dying on this street it will be cold by morning.

I will be cold by morning.

I blink. I can see stars through the smoke—too many to ever count, millions and millions. What are they thinking as they look

1

down? Perhaps they're sad because Paris is burning. Because so many good people are dead.

The stars . . . They've always felt like my friends. They're like tiny, shining faces I've known all my life. When I've been scared or can't sleep, they've been there to keep me company. I've done so many bad things in my life but the stars always forgave me.

I whisper to them now: "Can you hear me? I'm so scared. Please don't let it hurt so much . . ." But how can they stop me bleeding? No one can.

Please . . . My eyes fill with tears.

What will stop the pain? And how can I stop being afraid? I don't want to die. Not tonight, and not like this.

Maybe it'll help to think of happy times and the beautiful things in my life? I close my eyes very tightly. Yes, that's better . . . I can see a bird singing. A peach tree. A full moon over the rooftops of Paris. A rainbow. My brother's freckled face. Flowers in hedgerows that made the lane smell lovely.

And him.

I open my eyes.

Him. Marius. Yes, I'll think of Marius because he makes me happy. He always has, from the first time I saw him in the Gorbeau tenement. He's kind and shy, and he hums without knowing it and once he held my hand on a sunlit street . . .

Is he near me? Is that him, shouting, "Is anyone alive?" I try to sit up, to call out, but I can't, for the pain is like a fire, shooting through me.

Instead I whisper, "Stars? Bring him to me?" He'd make this hurt less, I know. He'd smile very gently. He'd crouch down and say, "Shh, Eponine . . . I'm here, see?" I don't think I'd be frightened of dying if he was by my side.

The nearby church clock is chiming—eleven times. My teeth are chattering. I'm so tired, so cold.

I close my eyes again. For a moment I see Cosette.

Then I see rain. It's rain through a window. There are ditches full of water. I can see a horse too and she's so wet she's turned from gray to black.

Where's my mother? Downstairs . . .

My body lies in a Paris street, surrounded by corpses and my own blood and a burning barricade, but my head and its thoughts are in Montfermeil. How old am I, in Montfermeil? I'm three. And I'm in a blue pinafore, watching the rain.

What did I know back then? Some things. But I didn't know, couldn't even imagine, the life that lay ahead for me or that I'd ever fall in love. Or that I'd put my hand in front of a soldier's gun to save that boy's life, and bleed to death for him.

BOOK
ONE

MONTFERMEIL

I was born in the year of 1815. That was a hard year. In the summer they had a battle called Waterloo and all the village's men fought in it, far away. There weren't many left in Montfermeil to cut the hay or bale it, to wring the necks of chickens or shoe horses or chop wood.

"I was walking," Maman told me. "Then I felt you coming. The grass was waist-high so I just squatted down in it . . ."

That was my arrival. While Papa was fighting in a muddy field, my mother was cursing. She pushed me out into thistles and hay.

"You were a girl—so of course I kept you," she said.

She never liked boys.

After the battle, Papa came back. Many men didn't return but he did. He didn't have a scratch on him and he clinked with coins that he'd stolen from the pockets of dying men. Once, he told me about it: picking his teeth, he said, "I pretended I was helping them but I wasn't! Ha! I was taking their pennies and silver crosses . . . Well, the dead don't need money, do they?"

That was my father. Luc Thenardier. Thin with a graying, bristled chin. His eyes were quick like a rat's—quick and cunning and black. He smoked a pipe. It yellowed the ends of his fingers and left a dent in his lip.

The Battle of Waterloo made him rich. With dead men's money he bought himself a new hat and a pocket watch. For Maman he bought a cape edged with fur. I'm not sure what he thought of me, his new baby daughter—but I know what he thought of the empty inn in Montfermeil. It sat at the end of the ruelle du Boulanger. Maman told me how they walked there one summer's evening, arm in arm, to look at it. It was damp and crooked. Its windows were greenish with moss; birds and spiders nested in its eaves.

Papa rubbed his chin and said, "Why don't we buy it, *ma chère?*"

She scowled. "Buy it? Why? It's falling down!"

"It is. But there aren't any other inns for miles and miles! People would come! And there's money to be made from drunken men . . ."

So they picked the moss from its glass with their fingernails and swept the bigger spiders out into the yard.

My father called the inn the Sergeant of Waterloo. "Named," he told his customers, "after myself, and my own brave role in the battle . . ." Papa told lies all the time and Maman would listen to them, polishing glasses and admiring him—this man who'd plucked buttons from dying soldiers' coats and then left those men to die in the rain.

My parents.

This inn was my home. I was born in a bright hayfield but I grew up in a dark, stone tavern with nettles by its door. Its sign creaked back and forth. Mice scurried behind my bedroom wall at night.

I think I remember my sister being born; it was October when the leaves were crispy brown. But my first proper memory came when I was three. It's clear and real, like cupped water.

It begins with water too—weeks and weeks of it.

A Month of Rain

"It always rains in March," said Maman. "Don't sulk. It'll stop soon enough."

But it didn't. For weeks, it drummed on the windows and turned the ditches to mud. The old nag's drinking trough was filled to the brim. "Poor horse," I whispered to myself because she was so wet she'd changed color. She shivered, ears back.

All the fields flooded. From my bedroom window, I saw the drooping apple trees and Monsieur Fournier's cows huddling on higher ground. The farmers couldn't grow their barley or corn in such wet earth: it ran, like wormy soup, through their hands. They'd shake their heads, very sadly. Then they'd trudge into our inn and stare into their drinks with a sigh.

Fires hissed with soggy wood. Water dripped off the brims of hats.

"A dry village? Ha!" Papa sucked on his pipe. "But still, the rain has advantages. They leave their wet coats by the fire to dry so it's much easier to pick their pockets . . ." He gave a soft cackle. "Always a penny or two."

*　　*　　*

Montfermeil was a small woodland village, seventeen miles east of Paris. It had a few grand houses with balconies but mostly it was made of little huts where the poorer people lived. Like Madame Cou, who talked to herself, and Blind Roland with his milky eyes. At the cottage with two chimneys lived Monsieur and Madame Lefevre, who were always side by side, just like their chimneys. They held hands and sang to each other.

"Disgusting," Papa called them. "Lovesick idiots . . ."

There was also a butcher's shop and a blacksmith's shed and a church with a graveyard where the Widow Amandine knelt every day. At the edge of the village was Old Auguste's house and he had a tree with sweet, juicy peaches. The bees loved that fruit as much as I did. In the summer, his tree hummed.

Montfermeil sat on the top of a hill. A road ran through it—the road between Livry and Chelles. But no river or stream could reach all the way up to us so we didn't have any choice except to walk with our buckets to get water. Deep in the tangled woods, there was a spring. Mostly, we paid old Père Six-Fours to fetch the water for us but he was crooked and spilled more than he carried. He stumbled over tree roots and wouldn't work at night.

Maman didn't like him. "He's useless," she said. "You'll be fetching the water yourself, when you're older, Eponine. Understand?"

I nodded but felt frightened. They said the woods were haunted, and there were stories of witches too.

So these weeks and weeks of rain were unexpected. When had

there ever been a puddle on each gravestone? A drip-drip-drip from each leaf?

Perhaps there'll be fish in the potholes and we can eat them, I thought. *Maybe we should build a boat?* I knew that Bible tale.

I was sitting by my bedroom window. There was a seat there—a small, padded shelf—and I sat with my knees pressed to my chest, resting my chin on them. My pinafore was corduroy, blackish-blue.

From here, I watched the rain. I watched the people hurrying through it—Claude the blacksmith, splashing, and Marie-Belle with her hunched back. The road-mender called Boulatruelle stalked by in a long black coat and I shuddered when I saw him because they said he'd been in prison for killing a man. *Walk past,* I thought, *don't come in here,* because I never liked it when he drank in our inn. He'd whisper with Papa, in corners. Once I heard him say, "There are candlesticks in the church at Gagny . . ."

"Silver?" Papa replied.

"Silver. The door's locked but it isn't strong . . . We could break it."

I knew many things. Where the blackberries grew in the autumn, and where raspberries grew in July. How my mother's face glowed when she found any shiny thing—a ring or gold or glass beads. She'd cry, "Look how they sparkle! Oh! Oh! Look!" I knew too that after Waterloo a man called Napoleon had been sent away—and that some people missed him, and wanted him back. Not everyone liked the French king. I heard Père Six-Fours mutter, "Was the revolution for nothing? All those people died—and what for? We're all still so poor."

Eponine. I was named after a girl in my mother's favorite book. Maman was broad and sly and her voice boomed like a cannon—but she liked romance novels with names like *The Beautiful Maid of Nanterre* or *The Queen's Lover* or *Secrets in Montmartre*. She'd tuck herself up and sigh as she read them. Her stories of beauty and love.

But as I sat on the window seat that evening I didn't know— how could I?—who was walking toward Montfermeil at that very moment, who was trudging through the rainy fields and lanes.

A Daughter's Task

"Eponine! Eponine, where are you?"

Maman's voice. Loud and demanding. It grew louder as she climbed the stairs toward me. Then she threw open the door.

"So! There you are . . ."

She filled the doorway. She was tall as a man—much taller than Papa—with fleshy arms and legs. She stood with her hands on her hips and looked about her. In the stairwell behind her, a candle was glowing; it lit up the sides of her coppery hair.

There was the single, impatient tap of her foot.

"What's this? Sitting? Watching the rain as if there is nothing else to do?" She clicked her tongue. "You've got work tonight, my darling." She walked over and took my hand.

I stumbled off the window seat. With my hand in hers, I was pulled from the room. We went down the creaking stairs, past the dusty corners and the black speckles that the mice had left behind. Past the cracked window—I felt its chilly draft.

"Keep up!"

Downstairs, the inn had only two rooms. One was the kitchen. It brimmed with frothing pots and pans; the sink was half-full of brown water and vegetable peelings and lumps of fat. Meat—hams, rabbits, pheasants—hung from hooks above my head. I didn't like this room. I never had. I hated its greasy walls and sticky floors, and I hated the cook who helped my mother sometimes—a sour-faced man who tugged the necks of hens and smiled when he heard the bones crack. I hurried through it. Above me, the rabbits swayed with their dead, glassy eyes.

We came to the heavy oak door.

Maman crouched. "Now, listen. The inn," she said, "is full tonight. Full! We have the rain to thank for that: The road to Chelles is flooded so carts can't get through it and even those traveling on foot would soak themselves to the knee! So here they all are, our traveling folk, unable to reach Paris and wanting a hot meal and bed . . ." She took my chin between her thumb and forefinger. "You know what this means, don't you?"

"Yes. There are lots of people."

"Which means . . . ?"

"More pockets to steal from."

"Yes! And what will you look for?"

"Coins, Maman."

"Of course, coins! And jewelry! Pocket watches, eyeglasses! Any fine leather! And I'm fond of embroidery, aren't I?" She spat on her finger, rubbed my cheek with it. "Be sweet. Be heartless. And what should you do, if they see you?"

"Smile very prettily."

"Or?"

"Cry as if they've hurt me."

"Exactly! *Très bon* . . ." She narrowed her eyes, leaned closer. "Now——go and find riches! Make me happy, Eponine!"

I walked into a room of roaring noise. There was shouting, singing, laughing; men spilling their ale and tearing meat from a bone; the chink of glass against glass, of metal against metal. A bowl was dropped and it broke and a cheer followed and a dog started barking and someone was coughing so loudly in the corner I thought he might be choking but then he paused, wiped his mouth with his sleeve, and drank some more. The hearth blazed and the pipe smoke pricked my eyes.

I tried to breathe through my mouth. I did this so I wouldn't smell the wet wool or the armpits. I tried to be careful where I walked: my heels went suck-suck-suck on the floor.

I thought, *Pockets. Look for pockets.*

Be heartless. You know what to do. And I did.

Before I could even talk, my mother taught me. When I was still a baby she showed me how to grasp a lady's collar and, like this, steal her diamond brooch. She told me to smile so that passersby paused to say, "What a pretty baby!" And as they did this, Maman hid their purse inside her skirts.

So yes, I knew what to do.

My first one was easy enough. I chose the miller from Chelles. He was already wobbling on his feet. He wore his apron; there was the chalky hue of flour on his beard. "I tell you," he said, "the Breton grain is bad grain . . . Seeds in it! Vetch, hempseed . . . How can I make good flour when there are"——he burped——"seeds in it?" He

16

didn't have any shiny buttons but as he turned, I pushed my fingers inside his apron pocket. I felt the cool shape of a one-sou coin.

Next, I chose an old soldier. He was dozing by the fire with drool on his chin. He wore fine silver buckles on his shoes and I bent down and plucked the buckles off, very quickly—*one-two!*

From a portly man in a waistcoat I took a pocket watch.

From the cowherd I lifted three sous.

There was a gentleman standing at the bar who wore a ruby ring. I saw its prettiness and I thought, *Maman would be very happy with that; she'd smile and stroke my hair* . . . How could I take it? In the end, I tiptoed up to him and shook his right hand. "Monsieur? Excuse me? Have you seen my doll?"

He looked down, blinked at what he saw—a tiny child with big, sad eyes. "Your doll? I've seen no doll. Little girl, this room is surely no place for you? And not at this late hour?"

"Perhaps my doll is upstairs." I smiled sweetly, let go of his hand, and moved on. The ring's warm hardness was pressed into my palm.

Maman was waiting in the stairwell. "So?"

I showed her. I held out my treasures in cupped hands—the buckles, the coins, the ruby ring. She smiled widely, her eyes as bright as the jewel. She slid the ring onto her finger and sighed. "Oh! So beautiful! So sparkling! Think of what we can buy with these things!" She put loud, extravagant kisses on my cheeks and said, "How I love you when you bring me such gifts! When you steal so well!" She stroked my hair as I'd hoped she would. "My clever little thief! My darling Eponine . . ."

*   *   *

After that, I took myself to bed. My sister was sleeping.

Azelma. A tiny bud. She was the little life who was, at first, just a strange bump beneath my mother's dress; later she mewled like a kitten in our mother's arms. Now, Azelma slept beneath a blanket with her thumb in her mouth. She made soft snoring sounds—pop . . . pop—and I looked at her for a moment. Then I took off my pinafore and climbed into bed.

The first word she'd ever said had been "Ponine." She'd said it holding her arms out to me, wanting to be held.

In bed, her feet felt cold. I rubbed them and tucked them between my own feet to make them warm. I found her doll among the bedclothes and warmed her too. I brought the blankets around us.

Like this, we slept so deeply that we didn't hear the cries of the soldier when he found his buckles were gone, or the miller's drunken shout of "Thief! I had a coin in this pocket and where is it now?" We didn't hear the rain stop either.

That night, the clouds parted. The moon came out. It shone down on our inn and on two tired people who were walking toward it—walking, walking . . .

Two people. A mother and her child.

Did they part brambles with their hands? Lift their skirts as they climbed over stiles? That's how I've always imagined it. They were always beautiful. Even in damp fields I reckon they shone as brightly as the stars.

Some people have that in them: a glow, a sort of magic. They're just different from the rest of us.

A Day of Sun

In the morning, Azelma and I stood by the window.

"Look! Look how pretty it is . . ." The fields were wet and sparkling; cobwebs were silvery white. The old rusting wagon that sat outside the inn glowed in the sunshine.

We heard a noise behind us. Maman cried, "My darlings! My pretty things . . ."

She was at her happiest but I knew it wasn't because the rain had stopped; it was because of the ruby ring.

"What a fine day it is!" She settled beside us on the window seat. "And what a clever girl Eponine was, last night. That ruby? We can sell it in Chelles for a hundred francs, I'm sure! And I'll buy you presents, my beautiful daughters. What would you like? Lace-edged skirts? Petticoats? Velvet ribbons?"

Azelma clapped, excited. She said, "Doll! Doll!"

"A doll? Of course! I shall find you the finest in all of France! And Eponine? Tell your mother what you wish for!"

I looked at the floor. What did I want? I didn't want rabbits hanging from their hooks, dead-eyed, or to have to fetch water from the haunted woods when I was older. I didn't like Boulatruelle, the creepy road-mender, whispering to my father in the dark. But these didn't sound like the right things to say and I didn't want to make her angry. Sometimes she called me an *ugly, ungrateful child.*

"To play? Can we play outside in the sunshine?" I couldn't think of anything else.

She frowned, like my answer confused her. "There's nothing else?"

"And a doll. Please."

"Aha! Of course! A doll for you too! With a porcelain face and a dainty hat! You'll be stealing again tonight, Eponine—and yes, you may play outside."

We ran into the sunshine, arms wide. We jumped in puddles together and scuffed through the soaking-wet grass, and I wondered if this was how birds felt, when freed from their cages?

At lunchtime, Maman said, "That old wagon that rusts in the lane . . . I wonder if I might make a swing from it? Would you like a swing of your own?"

That's how we spent the afternoon. She knotted a shawl and we swung from it, a cradle hanging from the wagon's arm. We swung beneath a bright blue sky.

I felt happy with Azelma's warmth against me.

Don't let this moment end, I thought.

I heard the woman's voice before I saw her. She said, "You have two very pretty children, Madame."

It wasn't Madame Cou and it wasn't Widow Amandine. I sat up to see who was speaking.

The lady was young. She was fair-haired and very thin, and the hem of her skirt was wet. She held the hand of a little girl—my age, maybe. This girl had fair hair too. She wore a linen bonnet but I could still see her hair.

I pushed myself up to see them better. Had I ever seen a beautiful person before? The only people I knew were gray and old. These two looked like angels.

I stared. I couldn't help it.

The little girl gave a tiny smile and I gave one back.

COSETTE

That night I sat on the bedroom floor with Azelma and this girl. The cat was with us too. We all watched the cat as she licked her paws with her rough tongue.

I asked the girl, "Why are you here?"

It had been a strange day. We'd swung in the cradle, picked flowers from the hedgerows and stuck them in our hair. Later, I'd seen the girl's mother kneel down and say, "Come here, dear Cosette; let me hold you." She'd hugged her daughter tightly and they'd rocked from side to side.

The girl sniffed. "I think I'm staying here now."

"Here? With us?"

"Yes."

"How long for?"

"Not sure."

Azelma frowned. She plucked her thumb from her mouth. "Why?" she said.

The girl was still watching the cat, who was washing the end of her tail now. "My mother's poor," she whispered. "She can't really work if she's got to look after me too. I think she's left me here for a while so she can go and earn lots of money. Then she'll come back for me."

Azelma tilted her head. "No papa?"

"No. He went away and didn't come back."

She began to cry, then. Her eyes filled with big, wobbling tears that spilled down her cheeks and dropped onto her lap.

"Ponine?"

I couldn't find a handkerchief for her but there was our doll's headscarf, which was a little flowered rag. I gave it to her. "Here. Don't cry. I'm Eponine. I'm four. This is Azelma. She's two and a half."

The girl blew her nose, still crying.

"What's your name?"

"My proper name's Euphrasie. But," she gulped, "but Maman calls me Cosette."

Cosette. A soft name. It suited her.

"Are you four as well?"

"In the summer."

She pressed the rag to her eyes. Her little mouth trembled. I wanted to help her so I said, "Don't be sad! Your mother will come back. And Montfermeil isn't so bad. See the window seat? It is dark outside now but sometimes, in the daytime, I sit there and see lots of things that no one else sees—like the cows scratching their bottoms on the fence, or Père Gauphin smoking when he isn't meant to smoke because his chest rattles and the smoking makes it worse. I've seen rabbits. I've seen Madame Cou picking flowers for her buttonhole, and people carrying the old nag's droppings in their arms because they say that her droppings make their cauliflowers grow. And in the summer there are swifts that swoop down the lane." I paused.

Her eyes were fixed on me and her voice was tiny. "Rabbits?"

"And raspberries. I know where raspberries grow. You can pop them on the end of each finger and suck them off—like this." I pretended I wore raspberries, like thimbles, on each fingertip.

Azelma unplugged her mouth. She laughed at this—my berries, made of air.

"See? It isn't so bad. And when your mother comes back you can show her the cauliflowers and the old gray nag, and you'll both be very happy."

Cosette quieted. She sniffed, stroked the cat.

Later, I took her to the little bed I shared with Azelma and lifted the blanket. I didn't know where else she could sleep.

I climbed in beside them and blew out the light. But I couldn't sleep at first because I felt too sad. Doesn't everyone feel sad when they see another person crying? When we want to help them, but we can't?

Be happy, I thought. *It's been a nice day.*

But I stayed sad. My sadness sat in my heart like a pebble—hard and sore. Slowly, I worked out the reason for it: it wasn't Cosette's tears, after all. It was that long, tight hug that Cosette's mother had given her, the way she'd pressed her face into the place between Cosette's neck and shoulders and rocked with her, left to right. What had she whispered to her? A promise or words of love?

I'd felt that pebble in my heart at other times, like when I saw people holding hands. When Monsieur Lefevre kissed his wife's forehead as she snoozed in the sun.

I turned onto my side in bed.

I thought how pretty Cosette was. She had apple-round cheeks and golden hair and her eyes were cornflower blue. My own cheeks were hollow; my hair was full of knots. I was only called *pretty* when I'd stolen things.

I slept in the end. But even in my dreams, I felt the tiny pebble in my heart.

A Drafty
Sleeping Place

In the middle of the night, the door was thrown open. The back of the door hit the bedroom wall and a lantern's light filled the room. Maman stumbled in. She smelled of gin and woodsmoke.

"What," she roared, "is THIS?"

She tore the blanket from us and pulled Cosette out of bed. She grabbed Cosette's hair and lifted her up. The girl screamed and Azelma started crying and the cat who had been sleeping on the window seat shot out of the room and my mother was hissing, "What . . . is . . . this?" as if she'd found a rat and was holding it by the tail.

Cosette squirmed in the air.

Then she fell down onto her knees.

"How dare you," snarled Maman, "share my daughters' bed? How *dare* you? Do you think you have the right to use our blankets, our heat? Do you?"

I hurried to my mother, said, "Maman?"

"Don't come to me, Eponine! What were you thinking? Did I

say that you could have that little louse in your own bed? Did I *say* that?"

"No, Maman. But—"

"Enough! *You*"—she pointed at Cosette—"downstairs! You'll sleep under the stairs, where the dust gathers and the spiders live. *That* is your bed—do you hear?"

Azelma sobbed but Cosette didn't. She just knelt very still, wide-eyed.

"GO!" Maman roared.

Cosette got up and ran downstairs.

Then my mother turned. "Eponine . . ." It was her slow, warning voice.

"Maman, I did not know where else she might sleep. She was cold—"

"Cold? What does *that* matter? Listen to me: that girl, she isn't a Thenardier like us. She is the bastard child of a slum-dwelling woman who cannot afford to feed her own daughter. Her mother is paying for us to keep her—*paying*! For her food and clothing! And do you think we will spend that money on *her*?" She bared her teeth in a cunning smile. "No, we won't! That money will be spent on *us*, Eponine. We'll use it for fine clothes and jewels and meat and *she*"—she spat the word—"will wear rags. *She* will eat crusts. And she'll do all the jobs I tell her to." Maman folded her arms. "What do you think of *that*?"

I felt afraid. "So I can't play with her?"

"No. She is our slave now—understand me? Don't show kindness to that poor, fatherless brat." Maman narrowed her eyes. "And anyway, Eponine, you should be pleased. I was going to send you for water when you were older, remember? To go through the woods at night? Well, *she* can do that job now."

She left, slammed the door.

I made the bed tidy. I looked for Azelma's doll and tucked her under my sister's arm. "There, there," I said to her. Soon she was sleeping and I heard the little pops of her breath.

The pebble of sadness was still in me. But I felt relief too because I was so scared of those woods where Boulatruelle lurked and witches lived. Now I didn't have to go there. It was her task— that *fatherless brat* (I tried out those words) who was sleeping under the stairs.

SACKCLOTH AND SILK

She didn't wear her linen bonnet anymore. Nor her ribboned frock or satin shoes. Instead, Cosette wore a sack from the miller's house meant for flour but that was too thin in places to keep the flour in. Maman cut two holes into the sack for her arms and a larger hole at the top for her head. "That," she said, "is your new dress. Not such a pretty thing now!"

Cosette did all the bad jobs.

She worked in the kitchen. Among the grease and black-bodied flies, she plucked chickens and scraped the scales off fish. She scrubbed vegetables and sliced fatty meat and wrinkled her nose at the pails of soured milk. When the cook carried rabbits by their ears—still alive, kicking—into the yard to have their necks snapped, Cosette cried for them. Then she scoured their blood from the kitchen floor.

She cleaned the windows and washed our clothes. She ate from a bowl under the kitchen table, kneeling on all fours. "Like an animal," said Maman, laughing. "Look at her! Just like the cat. She's so dirty, with fleas and thistles in her hair."

*   *   *

I didn't have to steal anymore. Every month, Cosette's mother sent fifteen francs: with this, my parents could pay for their tobacco and ale and gin and flour and milk and firewood and eggs. They could pay for a hock of ham instead of stealing it. I didn't have to dip my fingers into pockets.

This was new. In the evenings, when the inn was full, Azelma and I weren't creeping through the room now; we were sitting upstairs instead. Would Maman want us? It felt very strange.

We drew on the window's mist with our fingers.

We played with the doll and sang.

But Maman didn't come. Part of me was glad because I didn't like the inn being smoky and noisy and full of men. But part of me felt sorry too—because I didn't know how else to make our mother smile and say, *Oh, my pretty ones!*

Spring crept on. March became April and April became May. Sunshine brought the villagers out. Cosette stayed indoors, sweeping, but the rest of us came out into the flowery warmth. Marie-Belle, with her hunched back, sat on a bench and read. Monsieur Fournier's cows munched buttercups. Claude the blacksmith, seeing the sun, worked outside in the street and I heard the *ting ting ting!* of his hammer and the hiss of the shoe as he pressed it on to the horse. One morning as we watched this, Azelma and me, I saw how the tools on his belt were shiny. I wondered if I might take one, and what Maman would say?

Maman appeared. She stepped out of the inn in her prettiest dress, rustling as she walked. "How do I look?" she cried.

We left the blacksmith's and ran to her.

"Am I very beautiful?"

"You are! You are!" We clapped our hands.

"I'm going to Paris," she declared. "See these bags? They are filled with that urchin's clothes . . . Fancy, frilly nonsense. Her mother sent them, but that bug cannot scrub floors in such dresses, can she? So I'm off to Paris to sell them—and with the money they fetch I shall buy you far prettier dresses than *these* vile things . . . Satin! Silk!" She turned. "Luc? My hat."

Papa stood in the doorway. He tossed her a hat, took the pipe from his mouth, and said, "Get what you can—and more."

"I will." She kissed our heads—two smacking kisses.

At that moment, a carriage appeared. It would take her to Livry and from there a second coach would take her to Paris itself. She heaved herself inside it with the bag of clothes.

We watched the coach rumble away, down the ruelle du Boulanger.

Papa said, "She'd better come back with one hundred, at least."

"One hundred francs?" I gasped. "The clothes are worth that?"

"No, but she'll be doing more than selling clothes." He placed the pipe back in his mouth, gripped it with his teeth. "We know all the best places in Paris . . ."

"To visit?"

He laughed. "Ha! No, to *steal* from, you fool!" And he turned and went inside.

Azelma followed him but I stayed in the lane. I watched the

carriage grow smaller and smaller. I thought, *All we do is steal.* It seemed to be all we ever did or talked about. Wasn't there another way of living?

I remembered the hug Cosette's mother had given her. I looked up at the swifts, swooping.

For the first time I hoped for something better. For something more than Montfermeil, and this.

Paris. I knew its name. I'd heard it mentioned in the street as the carriage rolled by or as the blacksmith tended to horses. At the market in Chelles, they called, "The finest lace! From the streets of Paris! Come and see!" Madame Cou said she'd worked there once, as a dancer in a part called Montparnasse.

"Paris . . . ," she murmured, like she loved it very much.

Maman was in Paris for three days. Back in Montfermeil it was all I could think of. What was it like? I imagined boulevards— wide streets lined with trees that whispered in the wind. Tall houses made of stone, and horses that shone, as if polished. Men were handsome, tilting their hats when they passed a fine lady, and those ladies wore fox fur and pearls. Even the names of places sounded beautiful: Notre-Dame, the hill called Montmartre, the Seine, and the Champ de Mars . . . It felt like a magical place.

One evening I crept into the half-empty bar. My father was playing dominoes with Boulatruelle and some other men.

"Papa?"

"Hm?" He kept his eyes on the game.

"Will you tell me more about what Paris is like?"

"Paris? Grubby and dark. Alleyways to hide in."

I didn't want to know that. "I mean, are the ladies very beautiful?"

Boulatruelle cackled and Papa shook his head. "Not the ladies I've known! Let me tell you this: Paris is perfect for thieving in and that's all. At la Grève, for example, everyone's too busy watching the guillotine to feel a hand in their pocket . . . Ha!"

I felt sad: These weren't the tales I'd hoped for.

I knew Père Gauphin had been to Paris so I asked him instead. "Oh," he sighed, "it was a fine city once. It might be fine again but as long as there's a rich, plump king and starving people . . ." He coughed his rattling cough. "It's got its troubles."

Madame Cou didn't like company so I couldn't ask her.

Widow Amandine said, "Paris? I've never been."

It was Maman's romance books I turned to in the end. In them, I found my gentlemen with gold-topped canes and perfumed ladies who fluttered their eyes behind fans. Notre-Dame's polished stones reflected the sun. People fell in love on the Paris streets.

I sighed.

I laid down *The Beauty of Belleville* and looked out the bedroom window. It was my favorite daydream—that one day I'd be pretty, and I'd walk with a boy on the rue de Rivoli in a skirt that went *shush . . . shush . . . shush.*

Maman came back looking flushed. She stepped down from the coach in an embroidered cape that trailed behind her, and she smelled musky, strange.

"Maman! What did you see?"

She swayed up the path, past the nettles. "Where's your father? Find him. Tell him I have money . . ."

"And gifts?" chirped Azelma.

"*Oui, ma chérie*, and gifts."

I was given a shiny petticoat and a white fur muff for the winter. Azelma got a cape with a green velvet trim. She danced in it, singing, "Look at me, look at me!" Papa was handed a clinking drawstring pouch, full of coins.

Cosette? She got nothing. She crept out of the shadows that evening, as we were eating roasted goose.

"What do *you* want?" Maman barked. "Why aren't you fetching water? Go and get it!"

I stopped chewing. I thought, *Poor Cosette*, because it was pitch-black outside and she must have been so hungry. But she said nothing; she only trembled, nodded, and reached for the bucket. The goose tasted bitter after that.

I found her later. She'd fetched the water and was huddled on her bed under the stairs, whimpering.

"Cosette?"

She looked afraid. Maybe she'd thought I was Maman.

"Don't worry—she's sleeping and Papa is counting his francs in the bar. They won't see this." I held out my hands. I'd saved some of the goose for her.

34

She stared. "For me?"

"Yes."

She made small, soft noises as she ate. I saw the blisters on her hand and her flaking lips. "You've been asking people about Paris, haven't you?" she said, swallowing. "My mother knows Paris."

"Really?"

"She met my father there. She said they walked along the riverbank and he took her to theaters where the lanterns are made of gold . . ."

This was what I'd wanted. "Thank you."

Cosette wiped her mouth. We looked at each other and smiled. It was like we'd both given something the other person needed—a little bit of nourishment. Mine for her body, and hers for my soul.

A LITTLE KINDNESS

I sometimes think we're like the flowers—we don't need very much to grow. Just food, water, and light.

The hedgerows in Montfermeil were filled with flowers that summer. They spilled over walls into the ruelle du Boulanger so that they brushed the carriages that trundled past. The lanes were so colorful—blue anemones and pink roses and the tiny yellow daisy's eye. Nobody cared for these flowers and yet they grew. People gazed at their prettiness or stooped from their horse to pick a bloom or two.

Cosette didn't see any of it. She was indoors all the time, scrubbing the kitchen floor or darning our clothes. We ate raspberries and played in the fields but she didn't. In September she dropped a glass and it smashed, and Maman screamed at her, "You horrid, clumsy beast!" She hit Cosette so that she had bruises for weeks.

But she still had to fetch the water. "Off into the woods!" cried Maman. "Go! I don't care if it's cold or scary out there! And don't spill a drop, do you hear?"

Cosette wept very quietly when she lay down that night. I heard her.

By November, some nights were so frosty and cold that I worried she might freeze to death in her sackcloth dress, out in those spooky woods. But she always came back, shivering with cold but alive.

She was like the flowers in the lane, maybe—nobody cared for her, but she still grew, and she was pretty. Prettier than Azelma and me.

"She isn't a Thenardier," Maman said. "You don't want to fetch the water yourself, do you?"

I definitely didn't. But I didn't like seeing Cosette's bruises or hearing her little moans at night.

It was a wintry day when I decided to help: the fire in our bedroom kept us warm but all the other rooms were icy cold. Even the cat stayed near us. But Cosette was scrubbing the back doorstep. She was kneeling with a bucket of water beside her, scrubbing very slowly back and forth. Her skin was goose-pimply and blue. And at that moment, she knocked the bucket over. It clattered and its water raced across the yard.

Cosette wailed, "No!" and tried to dam the water with her hands but she couldn't stop it. The bucket was empty.

She gave a single sob. She'd have to fetch more water now and it was getting dark.

"Cosette?" I whispered.

She was all teary-eyed.

"There's a trick I know. Give me the bucket."

She didn't move.

"The bucket! Cosette, you don't have to go in the woods. The old nag in the field? She has a drinking trough. It's not good water because it's green with insects in it and people can't drink it but you could scrub a floor with it. The bucket, quick!" I reached out my hand.

I ran from the inn in my silk petticoats and climbed over the gate. I broke the icy crust on the water trough, filled the bucket up.

When I returned, her eyes were as big as saucers. I said, "When you're done, come upstairs. Papa is teaching Azelma how to cheat at cards in the bar and Maman is drinking with men so they won't know if you come up to warm your hands." I tried to smile. "I won't tell."

I remember how she crouched by the fire with her eyes closed as she soaked up its heat. Like the flowers that turn their faces to the warmth of the sun.

"Thank you," she whispered after a little while, and she padded back downstairs.

I liked being kind to her. It felt much better than stealing, or being mean. I was frightened that Maman might find out, but how could she? I thought my secret was safe.

But in the morning, Widow Amandine knocked on our door. She owned the old gray nag and, like the nag, she had big teeth and a swaying bottom.

"Monsieur and Madame Thenardier?"

My parents were suspicious. *"Oui?"*

"Please keep that eldest daughter of yours from stealing my horse's water. I saw her yesterday! She took a whole bucketful! It is theft—theft, I tell you! I pay Père Six-Fours for that water, don't I?"

"You're mistaken," said Maman, but her voice sounded tight.

"I *saw* her, Madame! And if it happens again I will bring the gendarme from Chelles and I'm sure you wouldn't want *that*." She snorted, turned, and swung her bottom down the lane.

Maman slammed the door and bellowed, "EPONINE!"

She found me on the stairs, seized me by the wrist, and said, "What's this? Taking water from a drinking trough? Did you? Answer me!"

"But you like stealing, Maman—"

"Don't be sassy with me! Why did you do it? It's Cosette's job to fetch the water—that horrid, bony thing!" She brought her face closer to mine. "Were you helping her?"

I paused.

"You *were*, weren't you? You were helping that stinking little . . ." Maman hissed in disgust. "Don't you remember what I told you, Eponine? *That*"—she pointed down the stairs, where Cosette was huddling—"isn't a Thenardier! Why should we be kind to her?"

"Because . . . it's nice to be kind?"

"Nice? NICE?" She kicked the cat as it passed her. "I shan't say this twice so listen well: Kindness is a useless thing. Useless! Do you think that kindness stops the guillotine's blade or the gnaw of hunger in a belly or the gray hairs creeping onto a man's head? Do you think a kind man's body won't be sucked by worms? Hm? These are dangerous times, Eponine, and people will steal and trick and lie and *kill*, if they have to. And it is the *kind* people who are tricked and fooled and stolen from! It's the *kind* ones who are murdered! Do you want that to be you?"

"No, Maman."

"Then be *cruel*. Cruel! It's what will save you! And"—she grasped my collar—"if you cannot be *cruel*, and if you cannot be *hard*, then I'm not sure you're my daughter at all." She let go, folded her arms.

I was shocked. "Not your daughter?"

"Maybe not. Maybe it's only Azelma who's my daughter, for *she* is growing hard. *She* does not help that snivelling wretch. And if you aren't a Thenardier, why must we keep you?"

I was frightened and I reached out for her. "No, Maman! I *am* your daughter! I *can* be cruel!"

She eyed me. "Can you?"

"Yes! Very cruel! You'll see!"

"You must prove it."

"I will! I will prove it!"

She sniffed. She bent down and kissed my head. "Good."

I wondered, then, what kind of flower I was because I drank up my mother's kiss like it was water. As if it hadn't rained for months.

"Promise me?"

"I promise. I'll be hard and cruel."

BEING CRUEL

I wasn't kind to Cosette again. I'd promised Maman I'd be hard and cruel, and so I was.

I watched how Maman did it, for being cruel was easy to her. She'd push Cosette as she passed her and call her names. She'd look at the newly scrubbed floor and say, "It's filthy! Scrub that again!" Or she'd point at the bleeding cracks on Cosette's heels and call out, "A cow! A cow! Look, she has hooves!"

"A cow would be more useful," said Papa, through his pipe.

I began with tiny things. I called her ugly, or I'd stomp on the stairs when she was sleeping. I waited until she'd finished mopping the floor and then I walked across it in my muddy shoes, saying, "Oops . . ." in a very casual way. I also told Cosette that her mother was probably much happier without her—"Maybe she's never coming back?"—and this made Cosette cry. Maman overheard this; she smiled at me.

As for Azelma, she soon stopped sucking her thumb and started sucking her meat instead, licking her plate. By the time she was six she could burp like a man. She'd run to Papa even though he had a horrible bristly chin and a smelly mouth, and say, "Papa, show me how to . . . ?" She wanted to know how to fill liquor bottles with water and cheat at dominoes. He showed her, saying, "What a fine crook you're becoming!" and Azelma squirmed with delight.

She was very cruel too. She hid Cosette's blanket when snow was due and threw stones at her. She started eating her food very lavishly, licking her lips and singing out, "Oh, this duck is delicious, Maman! So rich and tasty! Cosette, how is your blackened bread?" or "How is your apple with worms in?" Maman laughed and coddled Azelma, saying, "Well done, my darling—well done."

Maybe it was because we ate too much or threw too many logs on the fire but as the months slipped by, so did the money.

Maman tried to save. She'd tell Cosette to darn a torn bodice instead of buying a new one. She used fewer candles and less powder on her face and she raged at the cost of things—milk from Monsieur Fournier or a sack of flour. "*How* much? They should be ashamed! Robbery, that is . . ."

I said, "Does that ugly pig under the stairs need three pieces of bread a day? Let's give her two because that's more bread for us."

Maman's eyes shone. "Good girl, Eponine . . ."

But it got worse. The small white envelopes that Cosette's mother sent every month with fifteen francs inside stopped coming. Papa stamped his foot. "Where the *hell* is this month's money from that brat's mother?"

Maman muttered, "She's stopped paying."

"What? Write to her! Demand that she pays! Tell her that—what's her name? Colette?—is ill and needs fifty francs for medicine or she'll die! That should do it."

But it didn't. Maman wrote letters but no money came.

"Maybe she's died herself," she muttered. "How selfish *that* would be . . . How are we meant to buy petticoats if that yellow-haired strumpet is dead?"

So it was back to thieving. Azelma and I were given orders: "Out, out! Steal what you can, my darling ones . . ."

I went to the market at Chelles. It was a noisy place with dancing girls and fortune-tellers and a pig roasting on a spit and it was easy to steal from here—buttons, purses, and a jar of honey. I went to Claude the blacksmith too. He didn't have much money but he had a fine glossy horse tied up outside and I thought, *Such a horse must belong to a very rich man . . .* I slipped my hand into its saddlebags and found a bone-handled knife. It might be useful one day.

I wanted to make Maman happy so I stole whatever I could, and from everyone. One Sunday, I stole from church. People wear their best clothes to church after all, and I stole a cross-shaped brooch, a lace-edged handkerchief, and some white gloves. As Widow Amandine knelt beside her husband's grave, I unclasped her necklace and ran home with it thinking, *Maman will be so pleased with me!*

I stole from Blind Roland too. He was standing in the street and his eyes were open but I knew he couldn't see. He called,

"Who's there? Please talk to me? I'm blind and can't see you!" His wedding ring was on his finger. His wife had died in childbirth, many years before.

I tugged the ring off, ran away.

"Come back! Please, come back! Not my wedding ring!" But I didn't stop running. *Be heartless*, Maman had told me, and I'd vowed to be hard and cruel.

"Oh, clever Eponine!" she said. But I couldn't sleep that night, thinking about poor Blind Roland and poor Widow Amandine. When I went downstairs for a glass of water, I tripped over Cosette. She gasped, sat up.

"Eponine," she whispered, "is it true? Did you steal the wedding ring from that poor blind man?"

My belly knotted with shame. I almost said, *Yes . . . yes, it's true and I feel awful about it*—but I'd promised Maman, so I put my hands on my hips and said, "Yes, it's true. So what?" I spat at her, kicked her, and walked away.

It was a horrible thing to do. That wedding ring was all Blind Roland had left to touch of his wife. He used to turn that ring over and over and kiss it, pretending the ring was her. I heard his cries of desperation again: "Come back! I beg you! Not my wedding ring!"

I felt so ashamed. The next day, I wanted to be alone so I hid behind a stone wall where the roses grew in summer. It was September now but a few roses were still out.

As I sat, I heard voices. It was Monsieur and Madame Lefevre, who lived in the house with two chimneys side by side, as they always were. They couldn't see me because I was hidden but I could hear them talking.

"Every day, I love you more," said Monsieur Lefevre. There was the neat pop of a rose being picked. "For you."

"Oh, Gustave . . . And I love you too."

I heard them kiss and then they walked on.

Afterward, I wrapped my arms around my shins and I cried. I felt so sad because of the blind man and Widow Amandine, but also because the pebble in my heart was back going knock, knock, knock. Why didn't I have someone to pick a rose for me, or someone to say they loved me and always would?

I wiped my eyes. I looked out, across the fields. I couldn't see Paris but I knew it was there, with its theaters and happy people.

One day I'll go there, I told myself. I'd find love on the streets of Paris, and I wouldn't steal, and my heart wouldn't feel pebble-sore.

That was what I wanted more than anything.

The stars smiled quietly as I made my way home.

GAVROCHE

We grew thinner. Even with our pickings, our petticoats slipped from our waists and our bodices started to sag. We couldn't pay the cook anymore so he left, cursing us. "You're a bunch of stinking, brainless thieves!" he snapped.

"We are not brainless," Maman snapped back.

She sold the widow's necklace and her own pearl earrings and my white fur muff. She nearly sold the bone-handled knife but Papa stopped her. "Sell it?" He shook his head. "But it's so sharp, and it's pocket-sized . . . I reckon I've got use for that."

Only one person didn't grow thinner that autumn and that was Maman. She actually grew fatter, sucking the marrow out of bones and licking the stones of fruit, and she was bad-tempered too.

One day she slapped Cosette so hard that Cosette struck the doorframe as she fell. "Have you killed her?" I whispered, frightened.

"Of course I haven't killed her . . . What a stupid question!" But Cosette's nose bled and bled.

Then one night Maman stopped on the stairs. She groaned, felt her belly with her hands. "It's coming."

"What is?" asked Azelma.

"The baby," said Maman. "My God, this thing had better be a girl . . . ," she muttered to herself.

It wasn't. It was a boy. We knew he'd been born from the sound of our mother's wild screeching in the middle of the night.

"A boy? A BOY?! What the hell do I want with a wretched *boy*?!"

I hurried downstairs to find my little brother lying on the floor, waving his fists as he wailed and wailed.

Maman was hunched by the fire. She was sweaty and red and drinking gin. "A *boy*!" she spat out like a seed.

"We can't leave him on the floor," I whispered.

"Yes, we can." Maman stood up. "I'm going to bed."

"But he's hungry, Maman! And he's so little . . ."

"He's a *boy*, Eponine. I didn't want one of *them*."

I didn't understand her so I said, "Papa? Are you there? What shall we do with the baby?"

He came out of the shadows and shrugged. "I reckon we leave him. One less mouth to feed."

As for Azelma, she was seven years old and as hard as a fist. "A boy? I agree—I don't like boys."

With that, they all went upstairs, leaving the baby and me.

"Poor, poor baby . . ." I lifted him. He was smaller than our cat and smaller than the rabbits that used to hang on hooks. I rocked him a little. I said, "Don't cry, little man." But he wouldn't soothe.

Then I saw her.

Cosette stepped out of the darkness, as pale as a ghost. "He needs milk," she whispered. "And to be warm."

I thought of being cruel, of saying, *And what would you know? You're stupid and ugly* . . . But I didn't want to. The baby was so tiny and helpless, and I didn't know how to help him. "Milk? Here, will you take him?" I passed him to Cosette. "I'll look in the cellar."

That's where we kept milk because it was so cold. I felt in the darkness. There was one pail of milk and I filled a cup from it.

Cosette was singing, under her breath, when I came back up.

"I have milk."

"How cold is it? Maybe we should warm it—until it's as warm as a person is?"

So we placed it in the embers of the fire, for a while. We sat with the baby, singing to him. Cosette had a voice like a songbird—a thrush or a lark.

"Why doesn't Madame Thenardier want him?" she asked. "Why did she want a girl, not a boy?"

I shrugged. "I don't know. But she's always hated boys. I know she had two brothers and they used to beat her. Her father beat her too."

Cosette sniffed. "That makes me sad."

"It does?" She was sorry for Maman? The little prisoner felt sorry for the big prison guard? In the fire's glow, Cosette looked very pretty.

We fed him together. We dipped our fingers in the warm milk and popped our fingers in the baby's mouth and he sucked like a fish—*suck-suck*. He kept moving his arms too, and I wondered if he might be a fighter when he was older—a strong little man.

Upstairs, we found a crib. Because Maman had hoped for a girl she'd put a lace-edged blanket on it. We tucked him under this laciness and put kisses on his forehead, and Cosette padded down to her own bed.

We didn't talk about it again. In the morning, Azelma yawned and asked if there was any bread to eat; Cosette was told to mop the floor where the baby had been born—"and do it properly! Understand?"

Nobody mentioned him. He only survived in those first few months because we chose to help him—Cosette and me. When nobody was looking, we dipped our fingers into milk. We took turns to wash him and made sure he was warm.

After a few weeks, Maman looked up from her latest romance novel. The baby was crying and the noise was annoying her. "Have we named him?" she asked.

Papa said, "Who?"

In her book, there was a character called Gavroche. "That'll do," she said.

So when I went up to see my brother that night I tickled his belly and whispered, "Hello, little Gavroche."

CHRISTMAS EVE, 1823

His first Christmas on this earth was very hard. The dead autumn leaves and sleet blew under the doors and the inn shook. The cat refused to go out.

I don't know if it was the sleet that killed her or her old heart but one December morning Madame Cou was found on the bench in the churchyard, as cold as stone. Her skin was yellow, her eyes frozen open, and a tiny icicle hung from the tip of her nose. Azelma tapped Madame Cou's hand to make sure: "Yep, she's dead." Then she whipped off the brooch and gold cross that the old lady wore, and skipped home.

"Dead?" said Papa, picking his teeth. "No loss. Strange woman. What did you get?"

The brooch and gold cross meant a little more money that Christmas. We had customers again, because people were drawn to our big fire and sweetened wine. A fistful of coins bought a turkey; Azelma stole a pudding. We gathered pinecones to make the room smell earthy and festive and dark.

On Christmas Eve itself, travelers came to Montfermeil. There was a band of them—a juggling man and an acrobat, a fortune-teller, a woman whose arms were covered in ink.

A man cried out, "Who would like a story? A sou for a tale of magic and wonder . . ."

We leaned out the window, amazed.

"Look, Zel!" I called to my sister. "Can you see it?"

A man had a monkey on a chain and we'd never seen a monkey before.

She giggled. Briefly, she was my sister again, all soft and girl-ish. "Will they make it dance, Ponine?"

"Let's go outside and see!"

The monkey danced for a sou and the inked lady could breathe fire, making everyone gasp. In the ruelle du Boulanger they set up wooden tables selling pottery and sugared cakes and fruit in syrup. On one stall, there was a doll.

"Look at that . . . !" Azelma breathed. "Oh, she is the prettiest doll I've ever seen!"

"What must she be worth?"

Azelma snorted. "Don't be silly. I am not going to *buy* her, Eponine . . ."

She spent the afternoon wondering how she might steal this perfect, blue-eyed doll. It was too large for a pocket and its seller was never far from its side—so how? Azelma thought hard.

In the evening, it started to snow. It felt like tiny cold kisses falling onto my face. I turned very slowly to watch the snow coming down.

From the bright lights and warmth of the stalls, I saw Cosette. She was hobbling away from the inn. She didn't look at the color or laughter or music around her; she just trudged, head down, with the bucket in one hand. She was heading for the woods.

"Brat," Azelma said, following my gaze.

"Yes. Useless thing." But I wouldn't want to be going to the woods on a night like this and I felt sorry for her. It was Christmas Eve, a night for families. I thought, *She must be feeling so sad*. Her mother, we all knew, was dead.

"I hope she gets lost and freezes to death," said Azelma, meaning it.

The bar was full when we got back. It steamed with drunk men, singing bawdy songs, and I knew Boulatruelle was sipping in the darkness.

Maman grabbed us as we came inside. "Where have you been? Go upstairs! Put on your finest dresses and tie ribbons in your hair. I want you to look pretty tonight . . ."

"Are we stealing?"

"Of *course* you're stealing! But you must be charming . . . Sweet-natured and dainty! Because it's Christmas Eve and you might be *given* money as a gift, if you're pretty enough."

We did as we were told. In our room we preened and hurried, stepping over the sleeping Gavroche.

"I'll steal from the whole sorry lot of them." Azelma grinned. "Will you tie my sash, Eponine?"

As I tied it, I thought of Cosette in the woods: she'd been gone a very long time. The night was drawing in and the snow was very thick. What if she'd fallen or frozen to death? Her eyes open, like Madame Cou's?

I glanced out the window.

She hadn't fallen. She was in the street, walking back to the inn. Yet she wasn't alone. A tall man was with her, wearing a top hat and a coat of dark yellow wool, black breeches, and buckled shoes. I looked for his face but couldn't see it because the brim of his hat shadowed it.

In his left hand, he was carrying her bucket.

In his right hand, he was holding hers.

I stopped tying the sash and cried, "Oh!"

"What is it?" Azelma looked out the window too. She screeched, "Who is *that*? Who is helping that nasty little rat? *She* is meant to carry that bucket—no one else! Wait till I tell Maman . . ." And she raced out of the room.

I sat by Gavroche for a while. He'd stirred at Azelma's screech, but I said, "Hush now" to him, and he soon found sleep again. I wondered why I felt so strange—was I scared? And if so, why? I wanted to stay upstairs but knew that Maman wouldn't let me.

Downstairs she seized me. "Well. A *fine* thing has happened. That nasty little bug has brought a man here! A stranger!" She narrowed her eyes. "I thought he was poor when I saw him because his breeches are threadbare and his coat is made of a dirty yellow wool, but he's asked for a room for the night—and is paying forty sous for it! Forty! So maybe he has money after all . . ."

"Where is he, Maman?"

"In the corner. He isn't talking to anyone. I think you should charm him, Eponine."

"Charm him?"

"Go and talk to him. Smile! Play divinely! Be dainty and winsome and *charm* the pennies out of him . . ." She paused. "You *are* a Thenardier, aren't you?"

I went into the main room. Azelma was already there, swinging her skirts and humming to herself. She tapped a man's wrists, said, "May I have a coin, Monsieur? For my Christmas shoe?"

"Your Christmas shoe?" It was Monsieur Venard, who had no children left. All his sons had died at Waterloo. I thought, *Clever Azelma, to pick him.*

"Yes, Monsieur. We put a shoe by the fireside on Christmas Eve. We hope that a little gift might be left in it . . . I love Christmas," she sighed. "I love my doll too, even though she is raggedy . . ."

Monsieur Venard's eyes shimmered and he filled her hands with coins.

I had no doll of my own but I saw the cat, in the corner. *Be winsome . . .* And so I lifted up the cat and petted her. "Little kitty," I whispered. "Little furry thing. You're better than a doll because you're warm and squirmy . . ."

Was I dainty and sweet? Was Maman watching?

At that very moment the drinkers parted and I saw the gentleman sitting there. His top hat was next to him. He had his back to the wall.

He was half-lit by candlelight and he was looking right at me.

The Man in the Yellow Coat

Three people changed my life.

Cosette was the first. Here was the second.

His eyes were black, like hot coals, and they looked far, far older than the rest of him, like they'd seen many troubles. But they were kind eyes too. And I felt safe, for the first time in my life, just looking at him. Isn't it strange? I didn't know him at all and yet I trusted him.

I felt like kneeling down in front of him and saying, *Sorry for all the bad things I've done. For stealing from Blind Roland and all the other things.*

But then he looked away from me, toward Cosette. She was crouching on the floor under the table, trying to darn our stockings with a needle and thread—but she shivered too much to do it. He smiled very tenderly at her.

"Well?" Maman pushed me. "Don't just stand there like a fool! Go and get his money!"

But I couldn't really speak or move. I definitely couldn't steal from a man with such eyes.

"Go *on*!"

Still, I didn't move. Maman didn't like this at all and muttered, "Eponine . . . ?" She raised her hand to hit me.

"Look! Look!" I cried out. "Over there! See? Cosette has got Azelma's doll!"

Maman spun round and shrieked. Cosette had put down the sewing and was cradling Azelma's small rag doll, singing to it like she'd sung to Gavroche.

"*That*," roared Maman, "is not your doll!"

The whole room fell silent.

Cosette trembled. Azelma charged across the room and tore the doll away, shouting, "Get away from her! She is mine, not yours!" She yanked Cosette's hair and Cosette wailed.

There was clattering and screaming and the table was knocked over and suddenly he was standing there, the yellow-coated man.

"Enough." He didn't say it angrily. "Does it matter so much," he asked, "if she should play with the doll?"

"It does!" said Maman. "She's meant to be sewing, not playing! And the doll is not hers, Monsieur—it is my youngest daughter's and that urchin touched it with her grubby hands . . ."

"But she's a child, Madame. She must be allowed to play."

"Play? Not her! She's a worker! She must work! She must darn my daughters' stockings. See how pretty my girls are?"

He stared at Maman for a moment. Then the stranger picked up his hat, put it on his head, and walked out into the snow.

*　　*　　*

The room hummed. *Did you see that . . . ? Who was he?* Papa smoked, scowled.

When the yellow-coated man came back he was carrying a large parcel, wrapped in brown paper.

"A gift?" asked my mother. "Is this an apology? For your interference in my family's affairs? I accept it, and forgive you . . ." She held out her arms.

"It isn't for you. I've nothing to apologize for, Madame." He knelt down to Cosette. "It's for you, little one."

Her eyes widened. "For me?"

"Yes. It's a gift. Open it."

Slowly Cosette peeled the paper back . . .

Azelma shrieked. "No! No! Maman, look! It's the doll from the stall! With the porcelain face! No, she can't have it! I want it! I do!" She stamped her foot and roared with rage.

"It's Cosette's," said the man. "And the doll is not the only thing that I will be buying tonight."

Maman folded her arms. "There's more? Ale? Food? A bed? Are you buying the whole of Montfermeil as a present for that brat?"

"I'll be spending the night here, yes. And tomorrow, I shall be buying *that brat*, as you call her."

"What?"

"I'll buy the child—Cosette is her name, I believe?—and I'll take her to a better life. It was her dying mother's wish that I do so; she asked me to raise the child as my own, as if I were her father. I have a letter from poor Fantine, saying so." He held up a piece of paper. "And so tonight is the last night she'll spend in this"—he looked around—"soulless place."

I thought, *Buying* her?

Papa stepped forward, took his pipe from his mouth. "Might I ask for the pleasure of your name, Monsieur?"

"Jean Valjean. Now please show me to my room."

I'd never seen my parents look so shocked before or for the drinkers to leave in silence, one by one. Azelma cried herself to sleep. When Gavroche woke, I cleaned him and sang a lullaby until he was sleeping too. But I couldn't sleep. I sat upon the window seat and watched the snow come down.

He was *buying* her. Taking her away *to a better life*, he'd said. Now I knew the pebble in my heart was envy. I was just a thief in a village with mean-hearted parents, but Cosette's whole world was changing.

Then I heard a sound.

It was the creak of floorboards. *Someone is on the stairs.*

I padded to my door and peeped out. Jean Valjean was crouching by the fire where we'd left our shoes for a Christmas coin.

A third shoe was there. It was a small, splintered wooden clog and he lifted this clog, placed something in it. Then, like a breath of air, he slipped back into the night.

I could see it from here. It was a Louis d'or—a gold coin, worth twenty francs or more. They were so rare that I'd never seen one before. It glinted in the darkness like a star.

Take it, I thought. *Steal it. Give it to Maman and she'll love you and praise you forever and ever.* And I nearly did. But it wasn't my coin. It was Cosette's.

THEIR SHAPE
ON THE HORIZON

The bells rang for Christmas morning. The world was sparkling-white and the air was so cold that my eyes watered and my nose hurt.

Cosette didn't really say good-bye. Perhaps she was too filled with other things—shock, hope, disbelief, gratitude, fear—to speak. She just stood, clutching her new doll.

For the first time in years she was wearing proper clothes. Valjean had brought her a simple black woolen smock, black stockings, laced boots, and a little black hat.

"Fifteen hundred francs," said my mother. "That's what she'll cost you. We're losing a worker and you must compensate us."

"Fifteen hundred." He passed the money over in a drawstring bag. To Cosette he asked, "Are you ready?"

She looked across at me for a moment. I felt ashamed for all the times I'd called her *ugly* or *stupid girl* and kicked her. I'd so much to say but I couldn't speak either. We just looked at each other and that was our good-bye.

*　　*　　*

I watched them leave. The others went inside but I stayed to see them walk along the ruelle du Boulanger, past the blacksmith's and the church.

They grew smaller and smaller. For a moment they were just two dark shapes on the brow of the hill, holding hands.

That was the last I'd see of Cosette and Jean Valjean for years. But I didn't forget how they looked—two silhouettes against the snow—and I didn't forget how I ached inside.

I wished I was kinder and I wished I was prettier, and I wished he'd taken me too.

BOOK
TWO

COSETTE IS GONE

I thought about her a lot. I looked at the hearth and the yard and the kitchen floor and remembered her being there. As for the man, I only really knew his name but I thought how safe and peaceful he'd made me feel, and I missed that too.

Nobody mentioned them. Papa counted his money; Maman cursed the unswept floor. I whispered to Azelma, "I wonder if she's in Paris now?" And she just frowned and said, "Who?"

The months rolled by. Spring came. Buds grew greener and birds sang. The fifteen hundred francs meant we didn't have to steal so we could spend time outside in the sunshine. Sometimes Maman and Azelma took a carriage to Livry's shops and cafés.

"Are you coming with us, Eponine?"

But I always said no: "I'd rather stay here, Maman." I'd take Gavroche into the meadows instead where he'd crawl and gurgle and play.

They'd come back from Livry with pearl earrings and ribbons, or slices of the finest beef wrapped in brown paper. "We'll eat well tonight!" Maman would cry, and for a time we were plump again. But it didn't last. Spring became summer, and my parents argued and threw things at each other. There was less milk in the cellar, fewer candles at night.

One lunchtime I moved my spoon through a watery broth and asked, "Maman?"

"Hm?"

"The money? That the man gave us for Cosette?"

"What of it?"

"Do we still have it? We don't eat tender beef anymore and there's no wood for the fire . . ."

"You think it's easy? Running a place like this? Would you like to cook the meals and do the work and care for two children? Would you?"

Three children, I thought. She always forgot about Gavroche.

"How old are you now? Seven?"

"I'm eight and a half, Maman."

"Then you're old enough to be told." She put down her spoon. "Your father gambles—did you know that? With the wretched Boulatruelle."

Maybe I did know because I'd seen them playing dominoes together. I knew that men made roosters fight for money behind our inn sometimes.

"He's always gambled . . . but these days? He took that fifteen hundred and lost nearly all of it! There's none left, Eponine. He's

been a fool, saying, *Oh, but I'll win the money back next time . . .* ,"
she mimicked him, then spat, "But of course he never has and never
will. Boulatruelle is the rich one, now—rich with *our* money." She
rubbed her forehead and sighed.

"We must start thieving again, Maman?"

She glanced up. Briefly, she looked sorry. "This isn't much of a
life for you, is it?"

Maman. Mostly she was hard and hot-tempered and she'd
crack a walnut with her fist or stamp on a mouse if she saw one.
But there were also rare moments in which she could seem gentle,
or nearly.

I stepped toward her, thinking she might hold me like other
mothers did. "Maman, don't be sad . . ."

She flinched. The moment was over, and she shooed me away.
"Don't be weak, Eponine! Just *steal*, that's what I want! Steal anything! From anyone! And don't give it to your father—bring it
all to me."

I wanted Maman to smile and kiss me and say, *Well done, my darling
Eponine.* So I went out to steal for her.

I took the brass doorknob from the butcher's door, lifted a
hat from a sleeping man. In Chelles I snatched a gold-tipped
hairpin from the glossy curls of a lady and she cried out as her hair
tumbled down, "Stop! Thief!"

Maman studied it. "A hairpin? Better than nothing. What else?"

It was harder to steal as the weather got colder because people were more muffled and doors were often closed. But one night I remembered a conversation I'd heard between my father and Boulatruelle, long ago. *There are silver candlesticks at the church in Gagny* . . . Churches had riches, then? It was our church in Montfermeil that I went to the next day.

A House of Quiet

I'd never been inside a church before.

It smelled of dust and beeswax. It was silent too: No one else was in there, and my breathing and my footsteps seemed to be the only sounds. The windows were colored red and green and ink blue.

I sat on a pew for a while. *Here is a place where people have been christened and married and laid in the ground*, I thought. *Good people who do not steal.* It made me feel like I didn't belong there. I was a Thenardier and this place was meant for better, kinder folk than me.

I didn't want to live a horrible life, full of lies. But what could I do? I had to steal because we had no money and we had to feed Gavroche and keep ourselves warm in winter.

I blew my nose on the hem of my skirt and decided something.

I will give. Yes, I had to steal but I would try—try really hard—to give as well. With each bad thing, I'd do a good one, because that might, just might, make it all better. I'd be kind more than I'd be cruel.

When I was back in the inn I realized that I'd never even looked for silver candlesticks, but it didn't matter. I felt I'd come back with something even shinier—my bright new idea.

The Flowers and the
Mended Door

I started with small things. I stole a loaf of bread from the miller, and then, feeling bad about it, I picked a fistful of blackberries and left them on his doorstep. I knew he liked blackberries because everybody did.

After that, it was flowers. I still felt ashamed of snatching the Widow Amandine's necklace so I went to her husband's grave and left some honeysuckle on it. I hoped it might make her smile a little.

I swept the church path of leaves. I stacked its hymn books, one by one. After I'd secretly stolen a metal fitting from a bridle, I took a handful of mushrooms to the blacksmith.

"What's this?" he asked, suspicious.

"Mushrooms."

"I see that. But why are you giving them to me?"

"There's lots of them near the woods. I just thought you might like some."

He smiled. His heart was a trusting kind. "*Merci*. Bless you, Eponine," and I remember that because it was the first blessing I'd ever had.

*　　*　　*

I got more daring in my stealing. I skimmed cream from the top of milk churns and pulled a fur hat off a lady in Chelles. I snatched the horse blanket that covered the old gray nag because I knew it would keep us cozy when winter came.

"A fine little thief, when you put your mind to it." Maman gave me her sideways smile.

But I could be a fine giver too. I did all the good deeds I could, without being seen. I lifted all the dead bugs and old leaves out of the nag's water trough, cleaned the butcher's windows with soap, spit, and my sleeve. I took down Monsieur and Madame Lefevre's washing from its line and folded it and left it by their door. One starry evening, as I passed the old cottage where Monsieur Venard lived—the man whose sons died at Waterloo—I heard his door squeaking back and forth. I mended it with grease from our kitchen walls. He cried, "It's a miracle! Listen! Silent! After all these years . . ."

I helped Old Auguste too. His hands were so gnarled and bent with age that he couldn't pick the peaches from his tree that year. *"Excusez-moi?"* I said to him. "Do you need help picking the peaches?"

He nodded, raised his hands. "Look at these . . . such useless hands! What good are they?"

"Leave it to me, Old Auguste."

All afternoon, I picked his fruit. I stuffed my pockets and bodice and skirts with them and carried them down to him. "You've got loads of them—look! You could sell them—ten centimes a peach? People would pay because they're so juicy."

72

As we sucked our peaches, side by side, he said, "But you are a Thenardier, *ma chérie*. They say that your family thieve and cheat . . . why are you being nice to me?"

I sniffed, looked down. "I want to be honest. I've got a good heart inside me, Auguste, I'm *sure* of it."

He leaned closer, smiled. "Like the peaches? Sometimes the speckled ones are the best of all . . ."

Maman was uneasy when I got home that night. "Your skirts are torn and sticky and you've got juice on your chin. What've you been up to?" But I didn't tell her. She'd be cross or she wouldn't understand, so I didn't tell anyone.

If Cosette had still been there, I might have told her, but she wasn't. *She's far away now*, I thought. *With the yellow-coated man.*

I realized then that I missed her.

Those were some of my happiest days, but they didn't last. Papa changed everything—and not through gambling or theft but through something much, much darker.

THE BONE-HANDLED KNIFE

A frosty night. We huddled in the bar. We hadn't had any customers for months so it was just us and the spiders, crouching in the dark.

Gavroche was nestled next to me, practicing my name: "Pony, Pony . . ."

Maman hissed, "Make him stop. He's giving me a headache . . ."

Then Papa walked in, pulling his coat around him. "I'm going out."

"Where to?"

"That's my business."

Maman raised her finger. "If you're meeting that toad Boulatruelle . . ."

He shook his head. "I'm going alone. All I need is this," he said, patting his coat pocket, and I heard the tap of his fingernails against the bone-handled knife that I'd stolen from Claude the blacksmith. He always carried it.

Azelma stood up. "I want to come with you."

"No, you're too young."

She stamped her foot. "I'm not too young! I'm not, I'm not," she said, until Maman slammed her hands down.

"Take her, Luc! I've got a sore head and I don't want her here in this foul mood . . ."

So Papa and Azelma walked out together into the frosty night.

Gavroche and I were sleeping under the horse blanket when we heard, *Bang!*

It was the door. What time was it? Midnight or later. Maman was standing in our room, saying, "Wake up! Wake up!" I'd never seen her frightened before. She pulled the blanket from us, said, "Get out of bed! Out, out!" and she rummaged through the basket where we kept our clothes. "You'll need your warmest things—"

"What's happened, Maman?"

"We're leaving."

"Leaving?"

"Leaving the inn and Montfermeil." She threw clothes at me— my stockings and my bodice and my thickest skirt. "Your father has done a stupid thing . . ."

I dressed. "What has he done?"

"He meant to rob a man but in his wisdom he used his knife . . . and a gendarme saw him! A gendarme who recognized him because he cried out, 'Stop, Thenardier!' "

I felt sick. "A man's hurt?"

Maman straightened up from the basket. "Hurt? He's dead. A bishop. Your father heard rumors that he'd be passing through

Livry tonight—gold in his pockets and silver in his purse . . . But the man had nothing! Not even a sou, after all of that! He's killed a bishop and we're running away with nothing to show for it . . ." She muttered a curse word. "Downstairs, Eponine."

With that, she was gone. I wrapped Gavroche in every blanket we had, lifted him onto my hip, and went downstairs. Papa was sweating, pacing back and forth. "You're bringing the boy? He'll slow us down."

"He'll starve if we leave him! And Papa," I said, thinking quickly, "Gavroche can talk now: What if he speaks to the gendarmerie? About all the other things we've stolen?" I didn't want him to be left.

Maman sighed. "We'll have to take him then. Ready?"

It was trying to snow. The flakes stung my cheeks and hands, and as we slipped away Azelma asked, "Are we ever coming back?"

"No," she replied. "Say good-bye to Montfermeil because we'll never be here again."

We hurried. Papa and Maman carried blankets and bags, Azelma had a loaf of bread, and I clutched Gavroche—and like this we ran with thumping hearts and our feet going crunch, crunch, crunch on the frosty ground.

We passed the old nag. We passed the butcher's shop and the apple orchard and the wooden bench and the blacksmith's and the place where wild roses grew. The church. Old Auguste's peach tree.

Good-bye, good-bye.

I thought of Cosette then. She'd left Montfermeil in snowy weather like this, but she'd been promised a better life by the man with the gentle face. What life was waiting for me now?

"Where are we going, Papa?" I asked.

He spat on the ground, wiped his mouth. "Woods, ditches, old barns . . . Places we can hide because they'll be looking for us. We'll move at night when we cannot be seen."

"Ditches?" said Maman. "I'm not sleeping in ditches!"

"You will, or they'll find us. We must hide for a few years, that's all."

A few years?

Papa looked into the distance. "But we'll get to Paris in the end."

I glanced back at Montfermeil just once. We'd left the cat behind and I wondered if she was watching us at that moment—five silhouettes on the horizon, clutching blankets and bread.

Nobody saw us go. Were we missed in the morning? I don't think so, but I like to think that people noticed when the butcher's windows grew dirty again, when no one cleared the church path of dead leaves anymore.

BOOK
THREE

THE RUNNING LIFE

I climbed walls and waded through streams and crossed fields by moonlight, and if an owl hooted, Papa shouted, "Get down! It's the gendarmerie!" He said he could smell their rifles. When the wind blew, he thought he could hear their footsteps as they came closer and closer . . .

Azelma complained. "Papa, this is silly. I'm cold and I hate sleeping in ditches and they're probably not even *looking* for us anymore . . ."

He grabbed her. "Silly? They'll put shackles on me, if they find me! They'll hang me or take me to the guillotine—and you too!"

She flinched. "Me? Why me? I didn't kill the bishop!"

"No, but you were *there*! You helped me, and you were seen! Oh yes, they've a set of shackles for you too . . ."

No one complained after that. Azelma stole her own knife and kept it sharp. She clenched her fists and narrowed her eyes and, like Papa, she believed every shadow had a gendarme in it.

*   *   *

That's how we lived. We were filthy and tired and hungry.

We stole, like always. I reached into henhouses for eggs and kennels for bones, and I climbed trees for fruit. As for Azelma, she became as bold and cunning as a rat, smelling out coins like a rat smells out meat. She moved like a rat too—very quickly, along the bottom of walls. She cut off her hair ("It gets in the way") and knotted her skirts so she could run faster, and she came back at dawn with all sorts of treasures—milk in a pail and a silver hand mirror and a pair of men's shoes for Papa. Once she brought a goose.

"A goose!" Gavroche squawked, just like the goose did before Azelma snapped its neck. We gobbled up that roasted bird like we'd never eaten before.

We were hungrier than ever. But I reckon it wasn't just the running that did it. We were changing shape, Azelma and me. Our hips were getting bigger and our bodies filled out. Maman saw this, said, "My babies . . . My two baby girls. You'll be women soon."

Not long afterward, I found that silver hand mirror. We were sleeping in a barn and I felt a hard, cold something underneath the straw. I reached down and there it was. I thought, *Why hasn't Maman sold it?* I knew it must be worth a lot. I lifted it up and turned it over.

The girl who looked back at me had twigs in her hair and chapped lips. There was dirt on her cheek that wouldn't come off with a licked finger, so it must have been there a long time. Was she sad? She looked it.

I hadn't thought of Cosette for ages but I did now. Even when she'd been grubby and thin, she was pretty. Now her face would be pink and clean and lovely. She'd have perfect teeth and all that sun-colored hair . . .

I will never be beautiful. Not like she was. My heart's pebble knocked against its walls.

I put the mirror down.

Through the barn door, I could see the stars.

"Will things be better in Paris?" I asked them. And they shone so brightly at me that I felt they were saying, *Yes, they will, Eponine. Yes. You'll see.*

THE UPTURNED BOAT

We ran for nearly six years. Gavroche changed completely—from a toddler to a boy who could sprint and climb trees. He'd got Maman's freckles and coppery hair but his nature wasn't like hers. He was cheeky and cheerful.

"Come *on*, Eponine!" he shouted. "You're as slow as a snail . . ."

Gavroche. I wrote his name in mud with a stick. "See? That's how you spell it." I showed him how to blow grass and tie knots and one night I showed him which direction was north. "See that star? It's the North Star."

But he didn't look at the star. Instead he frowned and said, "What's that noise?"

There was a deep rumbling sound and we followed it to the widest river I'd ever seen. It was silver in the moonlight and foaming where it broke over rocks and it was so loud we couldn't hear each other and had to shout with cupped hands.

"I'll tell Maman! Stay here!" Because I knew we needed a place to drink and wash ourselves.

We found a small and sandy beach downstream. Maman scrubbed our clothes in the pools there; Papa sharpened the bone-handled knife against the rocks, round and round.

"Look," called Azelma, "a boat!"

It was upturned and splintery. It had a hole in its bottom so it wasn't good for sailing in but it looked like a shelter, made just for us. For a while that upturned boat was our sleeping place. When it rained it drummed on the roof like fingers and the raindrops dripped through the hole onto my nose.

"We'll stay here a day or two," Papa said. But we ended up staying much longer than that.

One night I heard a *crack!* It was like wood had been snapped or ice had been trodden on. Father, Azelma, and Gavroche were off stealing and I was cleaning a fish of its silvery scales. I didn't know what the cracking sound was.

"Eponine!" Maman screamed out.

I dropped the fish and ran to her. She'd fallen by the river and her left leg was twisted underneath her. "My leg! Oh, mercy! Oh, the pain!"

I helped her back to the upturned boat. But that night, she wailed and wailed. She needed a doctor—but how could we find one when we were criminals?

Papa was furious. "What's this? You've broken your leg?"

"My ankle, I think."

He was disgusted. "How are we meant to keep moving if you can't walk? They'll find us! They'll hang me!"

She was furious back. Despite the pain, she heaved herself up and said, "Yes, yes—this is all about *you*, like everything is! What about *me*? Do you think I like this life? Sleeping under a boat, for God's sake? We wouldn't even be running if it wasn't for you and that knife and that vile temper of yours . . ."

They fought till daybreak. Azelma, Gavroche, and I roasted the fish and ate it on the beach.

Azelma said, "Maybe we should go on without her."

I stared. "Leave Maman behind?"

She shrugged. "Maybe. It is better than being shackled, so yes, I think we should."

Sometimes Maman scared me or I didn't like her, but she was still my mother and I didn't want to leave her behind.

"How long do bones take to mend, Papa?" I asked. "Is it a month? Or two months?"

"Even a week," he replied, "is too long."

I tried to make a splint for her broken ankle—twigs and rope. "Try that, Maman. Can you walk?"

But she screamed when she tried, saying, "No, no! It hurts too much!" Then I went into the woods and found a straight, strong branch to be her walking stick. She leaned her weight upon it and it helped a little.

I whispered to Papa, "We aren't going to *leave* Maman, are we? She's getting better now."

He kept sharpening his knife and said, "I can smell their rifles . . . They're getting near."

*　　*　　*

An idea came to me one night. The rain went *drip-drip* through the hole in the boat, and I suddenly sat up.

I felt the hole above me. It wasn't very big. Surely we could fill it? Maman and Gavroche were sleeping beside me. Outside, I found Papa and Azelma; they were creeping in the darkness, trying to catch a roosting bird and snap its neck. "Papa! The boat!" I called as I ran to them. "We can plug the hole and sail in it and it won't matter that Maman can't walk very far because the boat will carry us, and the river's fast-flowing so we'll be taken far away . . ."

Azelma sniffed. Her face was wet with rain. "What's downstream, anyway?"

"Paris. It must be. Because rivers run into other, bigger rivers, and the Seine in Paris is the biggest river of all," I puffed, out of breath. "Papa?"

He stared at me for a second. "Wake your mother. Let's plug this hole."

We used wet cloth and mud and moss, tree sap and horse hair, dung and old rope. We packed it very tightly. "Will this hold?"

Papa shrugged. "For a while."

The rain stopped. The moon was high and full when we pushed the boat into the water. Papa held it as we climbed in, one by one—Maman, Azelma, and I. Then I turned to lift Gavroche into the boat—but he wasn't there.

"Where's Gavroche?"

"Who cares?" Maman said.

"Gavroche? Gavroche?" I yelled.

Papa climbed in and pushed at the riverbank so that the boat moved out, into the river, but I still couldn't see my brother so I shouted, "No! We've got to wait for him!"

"No, we haven't," said Maman. "His fault, for wandering off . . ."

"We can't leave him!" I scrambled to the edge of the boat and tried to snatch at bulrushes to pull the boat ashore and I said, "Let me off the boat! I'll find him and we can meet you downstream . . ."

"The moon," hissed Papa, "is full! It's showing us up! There's no time to go back and look for that boy . . ."

"But what'll happen to him? He's only seven!"

Maman seized me. She said, "Look at me. Listen. We are slow enough with my ankle without being slowed down by him as well. And he'll be fine, anyway—he'll get to Paris, join the others . . ."

"The others?"

"Urchins—other homeless boys who beg and steal and live on the streets . . . Now shut up, Eponine, or we'll push you overboard."

I looked back—and suddenly, there he was. He must have been gathering moss to plug the hole with because his arms were full of it—and he dropped the moss when he saw us sailing away in our patchwork boat. Gavroche began to run. He tried to catch up with us with his arms outstretched and I stretched my arms out too, and I screamed, "Jump! Jump and I'll catch you!" But the distance was too big for him. The boat went faster and faster.

Gavroche slowed down and stopped.

He grew smaller. He lowered his arms and I lowered mine, and we looked at each other until he was out of sight.

Nobody spoke for ages. The boat rocked past villages and fields and waste ground. After a while the plug of cloth and mud felt damp to touch and water came in, around our shoes and hems, but all I could think about was Gavroche. We scooped water out of the boat with our hands, but I just saw his frightened face and eyes.

We swam to shore, in the end. We were soaked and shivering. There was a row of rotting houses. A dog howled. It started to rain again.

Maman said, "Well? There it is. What do you think?"

"Of what?" muttered Azelma.

"Paris. That's the start of it."

I've done bad things but the worst was leaving Gavroche. The guilt and sorrow made my belly ache. I kept thinking, *I've let you down, little man.*

But there was another pain too. It was also in my belly, like someone was pushing there. It made me wince and bend over in the street so that Papa barked, "What's the matter with you? We don't need *two* invalids . . ."

I wasn't sure what the matter was but that night, in an alleyway, I found blood. It was on the back of my skirt and when I touched myself to find where the blood came from, my hand came back bloodied too. What was this? I was frightened for a moment in case I was dying or had something bad inside me. But then I remembered the rumors that this was what happened to women—they bled every month, like the moon turns from big to small. Years ago, Maman had said, "Your monthly times will come . . ." She gave birth to Gavroche a few days later.

I cried a little in the alleyway as I thought of my brother on the riverbank—and for having this blood on my hands that I didn't properly understand. What did it mean? Did it make me a grown-up? I hoped not because I didn't feel ready to be a grown-up Eponine. I washed my skirt in a rainwater barrel, then tore a little cloth from a sack and tucked it under my clothes between my legs.

I wiped my tears away and decided, *I am just the same. I am still me.* I could still play with dolls if I wanted to and I could still look at the stars and say, "Hello up there . . ." But I felt wiser too.

So that's how I entered Paris: wet and tired, with a belly that hurt. But I was also ready for the city and all the things that I reckoned might lie in it—danger and beauty and love.

BOOK
FOUR

THE ARRIVAL

Paris began as a path through scrubby grass. Then a few soggy crops appeared and a rickety windmill and gravestones showed through the weeds.

Gradually, more houses came, with more alleyways running between them. Pigs trotted, chickens scratched, children begged, and people snatched at things. Two men started fighting and I said to Azelma, "Keep walking," because she'd stopped to stare.

The ground wasn't earth anymore. Instead, it was dung and bones and matted feathers and rotting meat and human muck. The smell was horrid. A woman shouted out from a window, high up: "Look out!" And then she slopped a bucket into the street so we got splattered.

"They throw their toilet buckets in the street?" Azelma covered her mouth.

No ladies in fine dresses here. The only dresses I saw were frilly, gaudy things that fit badly so that their chests were spilling out. Those women had painted their faces and they lolled in doorways, picking their teeth. Some whistled to Papa and Maman hissed, "Don't you *dare*."

"Is it safe to walk in daylight?" I whispered. We'd not walked in daylight for six years.

Papa said, "We're safer now. See all of this? These are our kind of people—vagabonds, harlots, pickpockets . . ." He smiled for the first time in a long time. "There are worse people than us in Paris, Eponine, and the gendarmes here will leave us alone."

We walked all day. Maman hobbled more and more; Azelma got blisters on her feet. We passed through the huge wall into the proper city, where the houses were much higher and the sky seemed small. It was still raining. Our dresses were so wet they stuck to us.

"Papa," wailed Azelma. "When are we going to rest? And *where*, because I'm definitely not sleeping in *those* ditches . . ." She meant the ones with human muck in them.

Papa said, "I've got friends in Paris. We'll stay with Babet on the rue de la Charcuterie. You'll like him, Azelma: he pulls teeth."

"Pulls teeth?"

"There's money in it. Rich people will pay a lot for a proper human tooth to fill a gap in their own mouth—a whole franc, even!"

"Useful," said Maman, "if we get needy. The girls have lovely teeth."

*　　*　　*

As dark fell, Papa said, "Here we are."

We looked at the house. Its wood was black with rot. Maman winced as a rat ran past. *Knock-knock* went Papa's knuckles on the door.

It opened. The man who stood there was small but hard-looking, like a whip. His eyebrows met in the middle and the few teeth he had were brown.

"Thenardier . . . Well, well."

Papa shook his hand. "Babet! It's been too long. You remember my wife, Josephine?"

He took my mother's hand (the hand that wasn't clutching her walking stick) and kissed it. "*Enchanté*, Madame! And who are these lovely ladies?"

"My daughters, Azelma and Eponine."

Babet cast his gaze from our faces to our feet and back again. "How old?"

"Fourteen and fifteen. Good stealers too."

"Oh?"

"Very much so." Maman beamed, proudly. "Azelma has taken earrings and brooches and a silver mirror, and much more!"

"And the older one?"

"Eponine? Perhaps she is less good at stealing but she can read and write . . ."

Babet stared at me. He gave a slow smile, showing his pegs and swollen gums. "And she's got other charms . . ."

We were given a room upstairs. There was a single mattress that smelled of drains; damp bubbled on the walls. All night, it rained—I listened to it hammering on the windowpane.

I thought of Gavroche. I thought of peach trees and the dreams I'd had.

Cosette too. Where was she?

"Welcome to Paris," I whispered in the dark.

THE CITY OF HER DREAMS

Babet's house was just like his mouth—stinking and wet. The curtains never opened and the fire was rarely lit. His candles were made of pig fat, which meant the air smelled horrid.

Azelma hated it too. She grumbled about having to squat in the yard to do her business. And there was a little hole in our bedroom wall; once I thought I saw an eye, peeking through at me. But when I bent down to it, the eye was gone.

"How long do we have to be here for?" I asked.

Maman sat on the stained mattress. She couldn't hobble far but she didn't want to stay there either.

"We need money if we want to rent a place of our own," she said. "We can't leave this horrible place until we have ten francs, at least—so steal, my girls! Pick the pockets of everyone you meet! Get us out of here."

Winter blew in quickly. In the rue de la Charcuterie my teeth chattered and my nose turned pink. I wrapped a blanket around me because I didn't have a coat and I packed straw into my boots to make them warmer. I remembered the white fur muff I'd had— long, long ago.

Rue de la Charcuterie was a poor street. I thought to steal meat from the butcher but blood was splattered on his walls and the flies were as big as my thumb, so I kept away. The people were drunks or peddlers or urchins or those women with painted faces and squashed chests, and they'd hiss, "Get out of my way!" when I passed them. Some talked of a man called Lamarque. It was the first time I'd ever heard of him: *Lamarque will save us! He'll make France a free country again! Down with the king, down with the king!* And most people cheered and clapped.

There was nothing worth stealing here. I needed to find the richer parts of Paris, the Paris of my dreams with gold and diamonds, with dance halls and handsome men and satin skirts . . . Did it exist at all? If it did, I'd probably find the deepest and fullest pockets I'd ever seen in all my life.

I must find it. But how?

At that moment a carriage whisked past me. The horses that pulled it were glossy and the wheels had gilded spokes and through its window I saw the flash of silk and furs and a lady's gloved hand, and I thought, *Follow that carriage!* Because surely it would lead me there. I turned left by the man who sold pigs' trotters and right by the charred tree stump. I followed the carriages on and on— down the rue Mouffetard and passage des Patriarches. The streets got wider as I went. The houses were grander than any I'd ever seen and the shops sold wonderful things—soap, flowers, china, sugared confectionary laid out like stars. As for the men, they wore top hats and had neat mustaches, and the ladies wore white curled wigs with their skirts rustling behind them, and I thought, *Here it is! Here is the Paris I've been dreaming of.*

Its theaters had red velvet curtains. Its music halls had lanterns by their doors. There were cafés and clubs and ballrooms, and a lady with little silver eyeglasses that perched on the end of her nose—and I thought, *What would Maman say, if I took such things back to her?* She might love me more than ever. We could leave Babet's horrible house.

I dipped into purses. I unraveled a silk ribbon and snatched a sparkly brooch. And even though I wished I weren't stealing, I was still so glad to be in such a place, and I thought how beautiful that brooch looked—like the night sky in my hand.

Cosette. She might wear a brooch like this.

I put the brooch away. For a good deed, I stopped to pat a stray and gently pulled its ears. The dog blinked, like it was grateful.

I looked toward the Seine, where men and women were walking arm in arm. I thought, *If I've found the Paris I dreamed of, then maybe I'll find love as well?* I hoped so. To be loved would be better than a coin, or anything.

THE PATRON MINETTE

Maman loved the brooch. She clasped it to her tattered bodice, saying, "Oh, see how pretty? Do I look like a lady?" But like everything, we sold it in the end.

Azelma found buttons, firewood, a fur-lined glove, and fistfuls of coins. "Paris," she cried, "is wonderful!"

I smiled because maybe she was the same as me? Maybe she'd seen its beautiful parts too? But she added, "People are so busy with politics or fashion or the guillotine that they don't see me robbing them! Stupid lot!" So no, we weren't the same.

She liked what I didn't—dark deeds and alleyways. She liked Babet's stories about pulling teeth from men as they slept, and she drank his gin, and one day she said, "This house isn't so bad after all. Maybe we can stay here?"

But I'd seen that eye peeping through the hole in our bedroom wall again and again, and there were spiders as big as my hand, and I wanted to leave the house more than ever before.

*　　*　　*

That was a very hard winter. It snowed. Like babies, we pressed ourselves to Maman in bed for extra warmth. Papa stayed downstairs playing dominoes with men I didn't know. They smoked and swore and made plans.

"Who are they?" I whispered. "They're so loud . . ."

"The Patron Minette," said Azelma. "Haven't you heard of them? They're in the house a lot—but then you're probably too busy daydreaming by the Seine . . ."

I bristled. "I don't daydream by the Seine!"

"You do. Montparnasse has seen you."

"Who?"

"One of Babet's friends, and Papa's. They are the best thieves in all of Paris—so clever and exciting. You should meet them, Eponine."

I didn't like the sound of them at all. But I did meet them before very long. One night I was alone in the bedroom. The others were downstairs but I wanted to climb into bed and dream of being fur-dressed and beautiful . . . Then Babet opened the bedroom door.

"The fire's burning bright downstairs. Join us."

"I'm fine."

"You're blue. You're shivering with cold. Don't be foolish, Eponine . . . Come down to the fire." He smiled, showing his gums. "I promise I won't bite."

That's how I met them—the Patron Minette—by the fire, playing dominoes. There were four of them, including Babet. My parents and Azelma were there too. That slimy, tooth-pulling man showed me a space near the fire with a sweep of his hand as if he were offering me gold. "Here, Mademoiselle. Warm your pretty hands . . ."

One of the men was like a monster—so big he had to stoop to fit into the room. His forearms were wider than my whole body. His name was Gueulemer and he grunted a lot.

There was a man in the corner who I couldn't really see because his face was in shadow. "That's Claquesous," said Babet. "He won't speak. He lets his fists and blades speak for him."

The third man was called Montparnasse. He wasn't like the others because he was neat and clean-shaven. He was young—twenty, no more. He wore pomade in his hair and a cravat at his neck and a flower bloomed in his buttonhole, which made me think, *A flower? In winter?* Azelma was looking at him too.

The men cackled and passed a flagon of wine between them.

"All this unrest must help," Papa said. "Everyone hating the king and fighting for *la république* . . . People are distracted, easier to steal from."

Montparnasse replied, "It's true. The gendarmes have far more to worry about than a thief or two . . ."

I sat by the fire and said nothing. I just thought about Gavroche, and hoped he was warm and safe. Maybe he was playing in the snow, like children do? I hoped so.

When I looked up, I saw Montparnasse was watching me. He didn't blink. He just half smiled and licked his lips as a dog might before it eats its meat.

They boasted all night long. Papa talked of the bishop's face as he'd stabbed him with the bone-handled knife. Gueulemer held out his hands, said, "I've strangled too many people to count . . . See how strong these hands are?"

As for Babet, he told stories of pulling teeth. "There's a man near Boulogne who collects them and hangs them on string around his neck . . . I've pulled the teeth of pretty ladies, too—although they're less pretty once I've finished with them!"

This made me feel my own teeth with my tongue as if checking they were still there.

Montparnasse's voice was so soft the room fell quiet when he spoke. "Do you know Sanson?"

"Sanson?" Azelma shook her head. "No, I don't. Who's he? Will you tell me, Montparnasse?"

"He's the executioner. He's the man who works the blade—and he gets to keep the silver crosses or gold rings that the jabbering fools bring out with them. Once the blade drops, he pries these treasures out of their still-warm hands . . . Well, I found where Sanson drinks at night."

Azelma gasped. "You took the silver crosses from him when he was drunk?!"

"I did. I don't think it's stealing if I'm taking what was already stolen, do you?"

The Patron Minette ruled the Paris underworld. They knew how long to hold a man's head underwater. They'd dig up a freshly dead body in Père Lachaise cemetery just in case it still wore a wedding ring. They used sewers to escape through or hide in—and as I listened I felt ashamed and angry.

I ached for something else. For something *good*. I thought suddenly of Cosette and the gentle face of the yellow-coated man.

Their hearts were the opposite of the black hearts sitting by this fire. Where were they?

I want more than this, I thought. Just like I'd wanted more than a life in Montfermeil. *I want to get out of here.*

I stole and stole. There was no other way to get enough money to leave the house on rue de la Charcuterie, so I hurried through Les Halles taking every shiny thing. I took pocket watches and eyeglasses and candlesticks with their candles still in and stirrups from saddles and a pair of lambskin gloves. I whipped a walking cane away from a man, took it back to Maman to replace her rickety branch.

More, steal more . . . I didn't even do good deeds as I went. I didn't have time to, for I just wanted to be far, far away from Babet's brown teeth, the damp mattress and the lice, and the eye that peered through that hole in the wall.

THE KEY

A blizzarding night. Hard to steal in blizzards because most people were indoors and my hands were too numb to do much.

I stumbled through the snowy streets. I was shivering and blue, but it was better than sitting by Babet's fire. Here at least I could daydream. *Perhaps I will be rescued. Maybe a handsome man will find me, say, "Why is such a beauty in rags and tatters? Come with me . . ."* Such little dreams kept me warm inside.

As I crept along the rue du Puits-l'Ermite, I saw something, bronze-colored, half hidden by snow.

I bent down.

A key. It was big and heavy. What might it be worth and could it be melted down? Was there gold in it? I ran back to the rue de la Charcuterie thinking, *This will get us out of there! We'll be able to live in our own house because of this key!*

Maman leaned on her new walking stick and said, "Let me see."

"Do you think it might be gold? Maman?"

"It's heavy, for certain . . ." She weighed it in her hand.

Papa and Babet came with their beady eyes and said, "A key?"

"Eponine found it. I don't think it's gold but it might be worth something. Feel how heavy it is."

Papa smiled. "Never mind selling it. Where did you find it?"

I said, "Rue du Puits-l'Ermite."

"Where on the rue du Puits-l'Ermite?"

"Near the lamppost that the dogs use."

"And did anyone see you pick it up?"

"No, Papa. It was snowing and no one was out except me."

"And is it still snowing?"

"Yes, very hard." I didn't understand his questions. "Why, Papa? Why must it be snowing?"

He started to cackle. "Because what do keys open, Eponine? Doors! I'm going to try all the doors on rue du Puits-l'Ermite with it—until a door opens and lets us in . . . And if it's snowing?"

"It will cover our tracks!" sang Azelma. "People will stay inside and no one will follow us or know it was us!"

They all came forward at that moment. Gueulemer, Claquesous, and Montparnasse stepped into the candlelight like ghosts.

"This sounds like a wonderful plan," Maman said.

"It does," said Babet. "What are we waiting for?"

I cried that night. I hadn't meant for a home to be burgled, for a sleeping person to be robbed of all they had in the whole wide world. I'd just thought Papa could sell the key for its metal, that's all.

I whispered, "Don't let anyone die. Please . . ." It'd be my fault.

They all came back at dawn. Under their snowy coats and in their pockets and carried between them they had tables, paintings, the poker for the fire, a carriage clock, and shiny knobs from the sleeper's bed. In a polished wooden box they'd found banknotes and jewels. Also, a letter in a woman's hand in which she had written, *"All I ever think about is you . . ."*

"A letter? No value in that," said my papa. He threw the note on the fire and I watched it burn.

I felt wretched, tired and lonely. The others drank and cackled but I stayed in the bedroom, hugging my knees. Downstairs, I heard Papa say, "Eponine? Oh, she's too soft and foolish. But she needn't be sad—I left the key in the door for him, so at least he has something!" And their laughter shook the whole house. I hated that key. It meant that somewhere in Paris, a man lost all that mattered to him on a snowy night. He lost money and paintings—but a love letter too, and maybe that letter was the greatest loss of all.

Papa sold everything—the bed knobs, the jewels.

"But we'll keep the table," said Maman. "We'll need it in our new home."

"New home?"

"We've got enough money now, Eponine. That key hasn't just opened a crooked old door on the rue du Puits-l'Ermite. It'll open the door to our new home too."

I gasped. "Really? No Babet and no Montparnasse?"

"No, just us," said Maman.

THE GORBEAU TENEMENT

Love. It's almost the smallest word I know. If it were an object, I might drop it or forget it because it's so tiny. But it's not a small feeling, even though it grows from a moment as small as an apple seed.

In my daydreams I found love in the smart parts of Paris, where the ladies wore ermine and music played. I never thought I'd find it in the gray and drafty stairwell of the Gorbeau tenement, but I did.

Our new home was south of the river. We trudged through the snow toward it, over the Seine, past the old horse market, and beyond the rue du Petit Banquier, where the tannery was.

"Where are we going, Papa?" asked Azelma, clutching her dress at the neck for warmth. "I liked it at Babet's . . . Why couldn't we stay there?"

"We're going to a place that Claquesous told me about."

"Claquesous speaks?" said Maman drily. This was the poorest part of Paris, where the homeless huddled by damp fires and where the slaughterhouse was. "Where are we?"

"Salpêtrière."

Stunted trees, crumbling walls. *It's like the end of the world*, I thought.

There was a long black building ahead of us. "There," said Papa. "That's our new home."

The Gorbeau tenement had row upon row of windows that peered out like eyes. A single door stood, mouthlike. I thought it looked like a skull.

"The rent's cheap," Papa said. "It'll do."

The landlady was called Madame Bourgon. I don't think she'd ever brushed her hair because it was knots, all over. She had the slow-moving eyes of someone who drank too much.

"Yes?"

"You've got a room to rent?"

She eyed us. "There are four of you?"

"Four."

"One room is four sous a week. A sou for each person."

Maman scoffed. "Four? These two are children! They are not yet in their teens! Why should they be a sou each, as we are?"

This was as clear a lie as if she had said it was summer outside.

The landlady cackled. "These two? Ha! Look at their faces! Those aren't children's faces and they've got the shapes of women, and"—she brought out a finger, pointed—"if you think I can be fooled by a liar, you're a fool yourself. Understand?"

So it was four sous and no less.

When asked for our name, Papa said *Jondrette*.

"Jondrette?" I whispered to Azelma. "Why Jondrette?"

"Everybody knows the name Thenardier," she replied. "After the murdered bishop? It's a wanted name in France and that old bat"—she meant Madame Bourgon—"wouldn't rent her room to us if she knew who we really were."

It was an echoing, drafty place. There were lots of stairs too because the corridors were so long that there were stairwells at each end of them. Most of the rooms were empty but some were rented by people who were as thin and poor as us. Our room was on the second floor. There wasn't much in it, just a single chair and two rickety beds. I had a window but it was so dirty I couldn't really see through it. There was a small hearth for cooking. A bucket for private doings.

"Well?" said Maman. "What do you think?"

I didn't know what to say. At least it was better than the house on the rue de la Charcuterie.

I hoped I might be able to stop stealing now. But no. Maman ordered it: "How else are we going to eat? Keep stealing!"

"But it's so cold outside . . ."

"Then steal some firewood to warm yourself afterward! Tsk . . ."

I crept through Salpêtrière, looking. There was nothing to steal. Even the trees looked poor because their branches had been snapped off for fuel. In the graveyard, people were sheltering against the gravestones and they looked as dead as the people in the ground.

Azelma managed to catch a crow. She carried it back to the Gorbeau, where it flapped and screeched until Papa wrung its neck. It tasted nasty but it was food. Its scattered soot-black feathers never really left our room.

"There's nothing to steal, Maman! People are poorer than we are!"

"Try harder."

Madame Bourgon saw all of this. She spied us as we came and went, said, "Always out walking, aren't you . . . ?"

From this, I knew she was nosy—and that if I ever wanted to know something, she'd be the one to ask.

I walked farther and farther into Paris.

Christmas was coming closer. It meant the streets looked more colorful and there was music everywhere. On the rue de Rivoli, people wore fur and long woolen coats and the lanterns dazzled me—but I also thought of the shivering folk in the graveyard in Salpêtrière. It didn't seem fair to have rich and poor side by side.

One late afternoon, I came to a square called the place Saint-Michel. I stopped because it looked so pretty, with candles in its windows. Snow had started falling again. The nearby clock tower struck seven times.

At the side of the place Saint-Michel was a café. Its windows were steamy from all the people inside it and so I hurried to it, hoping that it might warm me a little. CAFÉ MUSAIN read the sign. I pressed my face against its foggy glass. Inside was a roaring fire and dozens and dozens of young men, drinking and talking so loudly that I could hear them even though the door was closed.

"Vive la république!" cried one with golden curls. They cheered, and another boy with reddish hair raised his glass, saying, "A toast! A toast! To Lamarque!"

They all stood, glasses high in the air. "Larmarque!"

A boy with half-moon spectacles began to sing, stamping his feet.

I stepped away from the window. *Such passion.* I'd seen it in their pink cheeks and flashing eyes and I'd heard it in the way they spoke. What were they talking about? I didn't know much but I knew that the king was hated and most people wanted him gone.

Those men wished for a better life, just like I did. I was just one little person in a world of millions but I still mattered. I had hopes and dreams, like them. The thought kept me warm as I hurried home.

THE CHESTNUT SELLER

Papa was angry. "Nothing? You've been out all day and you've come back with nothing?" He kicked the wall. "At least your sister brings crows and rats . . ."

"Rats?"

"It's food! And it's more than *you're* bringing us . . ."

"She's too busy dreaming . . . ," muttered Maman, disappointed in me.

With nothing to steal I had to try something else. And I had a thought: *I'll get a job.* It was nearly Christmas after all, and I was sure there would be at least one shopkeeper in Paris who might need a little help. So I tied my hair back with string and scrubbed the stains from my skirt and I knocked on dozens of doors—butchers, grocers, vintners, taverners, fishmongers, the coffinmakers who liked the word *guillotine*, the confectioner on rue d'Estard whose window was one of the prettiest things I'd seen in all my life. The confectioner saw me looking through his window.

"Hey!" he said. "What do you want? Get away from there!"

I jumped. "Monsieur, I'm just looking for a little work. Maybe I could do something useful for you, in return for a coin or two?"

He did a single, hard laugh. "You?"

"Please, Monsieur, I'm a hard worker, and—"

"Look at you! Grime on your hands and holes in your clothes! There are folk in the ground at Père Lachaise who have more flesh on their bones! Employ you? I wouldn't even serve you. Move on or I'll make you." And he raised his fist.

He was the worst of them: his shop was full of sweetness but the rest of him was sour. But others were not that different.

The butcher folded his arms. "No work here."

"Not even to sweep the floors? Even if it's just for one day?"

"No work."

When I tried one vintner—maybe I could move barrels?—he narrowed his eyes and said, "Are you a royalist? Supporting the king? Or are you after a republic like so many are?"

I wasn't sure. What had they said at the Café Musain? I mumbled, "I think Lamarque will save us."

"Then you're a *traitor*," he shouted, "as well as a grubby little wretch! Now shoo, before I set my dog on you!"

For three days, I tried so hard to live a proper life. But I was jeered at and pushed away, and I didn't get any food to take back to the Gorbeau tenement. I was hungry and cold.

Then I smelled something. What was it? It was sweet and hot and my belly growled at it. On the corner of rue de Pontoise and passage des Patriarches, there was a metal drum. Inside this drum, I saw the reddish glow of coals.

A man stood near it, saw me. "Yes?"

My voice was tiny. "May I stand here a while? Just for warmth?"

He was roasting chestnuts. They were darkening and splitting to show their flesh. I'd have given so much to taste just one of them. I could barely find the strength of heart to speak to him but I said, "Monsieur, forgive me—I don't have a single coin on me but I would love to have one of your chestnuts. Are there any errands I could do for you? Any pots that may need cleaning?"

He tilted his head. "A single chestnut? Child, I can spare you a single chestnut. Come closer." He lifted a nut from his fire and held it out.

I was shocked. No curses from him? No *Get away from here!* "Really? For free?"

When he placed it in my hand it was almost too hot for me to hold—but I loved how it felt. Warmth! At last! He watched me as I ate. His eyes had a shine to them. "Mademoiselle," he whispered, "look how thin you are . . ."

I looked. My elbows and knees were the largest part of my limbs. I looked as if I could be snapped like a twig.

"How do you live?"

I wondered how to answer. Then I thought, *Be honest with this good man*, and so with the taste of chestnut on my tongue, I said, "I've tried for work, Monsieur, but no one will give me any. I beg a little. But I steal, most of all. I hate to do it, I really do—but if we don't steal, we starve."

The chestnut seller listened. I thought he might call me a name like *thief* or *scoundrel* and tell me to clear off, but he didn't. He just said, "You poor thing. There are many like you, I know. This city . . . We thought the revolution would lead to a better life but what's changed? Come closer, still. Warm yourself. And here." He took a twist of paper, filled it with many chestnuts—five, six, seven of them. "I've no job to give you and not much money of my own, but you're not much older than my son and far thinner. If I can ever help you, child, I'll try to."

I took the chestnuts, wordless. Seven of them? For nothing?

"A gift," he said.

"A gift?"

"It's Christmas Eve, after all." I felt like weeping. The vintner and confectioner had been so cruel but this man was so kind . . . The bells of Notre-Dame pealed across the Seine.

I remembered another Christmas Eve, many years before. The yellow-coated man. His eyes had been like the chestnut man's eyes—sad and very gentle. Suddenly, my own eyes brimmed and Notre-Dame blurred and I felt so thankful for these chestnuts and for such good people. I whispered, "Thank you," as I ran home under the nighttime sky.

My family gobbled the chestnuts up.

"You stole them?" said Maman with her mouth full.

"Yes," I lied. It just seemed better to, and as I watched them eat I thought, *There is still good in the world.* The men in the Café Musain had believed it and the chestnut-seller had proved it.

The next morning I said merry Christmas to everyone I'd met and liked in my life: Cosette, Valjean, little Gavroche, the Lefevres,

Widow Amandine, the black cat in Montfermeil. Merry Christmas to the stars. Merry Christmas to Old Auguste and his peaches. Merry Christmas to the upturned boat that lay on a riverbed these days but might be a home (or so I hoped) to fish and eels, and unseen river things.

WRITTEN WORDS AND SPOKEN WORDS

Christmas passed. The year was 1831. The man called Lamarque was being talked of everywhere. *Maybe this will be the year that he kicks the king off the throne? Do you think?* It wasn't snowing now but it was too cold for the fallen snow to melt so it just lay there getting dirty. There were yellow spots where dogs had been.

"I hate this weather," said Azelma. "It makes everything harder . . ."

I was tired of it too, but I could imagine Cosette in it. No sackcloth anymore. She would be wearing goatskin boots and a velvet cape and maybe a white fur muff like the one I used to have. Now it was me wearing rags.

"A new year," declared Papa, "needs a new plan. And I've got one." His eyes flashed excitedly. "We shall write letters!"

"Letters? What?" Maman didn't understand either.

"To the rich, Josephine! I'll write begging letters—the best that have ever been written! I'll say my children are dying and we need money to save them, or I'll say I'm a great artist in need of coins in order to finish my greatest piece—which I will dedicate to my benefactor, of course . . . Or I'll say we're good religious people who will bless any man who spares a franc or two . . ."

Maman started to smile. She liked this idea. "Or give the letter to those who love Lamarque, saying that we are collecting money for his campaign . . ."

"Or," chirped Azelma, "that we wish to help the poor, fatherless urchins of this city and need pennies to do so!"

"Yes! Yes! *Très bien*, Azelma!"

I tilted my head. "So . . . tell lies?"

Maman snapped. "Of *course* we'll tell lies. Don't be so prissy! There's no use in being kind, remember? Kindness gets you nowhere in this world."

So Papa wrote letters. And Azelma and I took those letters out into the richer parts of Paris like the rue de Rivoli and boulevard Saint-Germain. "Look poor and pitiful," Papa hissed, so we dirtied our faces and widened our eyes.

Near Saint-Sulpice, Azelma said, "That gentleman? Let's try him. Look how well groomed his whiskers are. He must have money. Also, he wears a crucifix so he is godly . . ." I watched my sister as she scuttled to him and tugged his sleeves. He read the letter she gave him. She even pretended to cry very daintily and I saw the whiskered man reach into his coat . . .

"Easy," she sang afterward, jangling with coins. "Your turn, Eponine. You've got the letters?"

"Yes."

"Then I'll see you later—back at the Gorbeau."

Maybe I was still warm from the fiery hearts in the Café Musain or by the chestnut-seller's kindness but I didn't want to lie, or dupe, or steal. Instead, I went to the rue de Rivoli, tucked myself against some railings, and just watched them all to-ing and fro-ing. I saw how a grand dame descended from her carriage holding the coachman's wrist with her elegant, white-gloved hand.

Beauty . . . Love . . . Two things I didn't have. I closed my eyes, wanting them.

Anything could happen. That's how it felt, in Paris.

At that very moment someone touched me. A hand took hold of my shoulder. My eyes sprang open because I thought, *It is a gendarme! He knows about these letters!* and I screeched, "Get off!" and tried to free myself.

"Hey . . . Ssh, now." It was a man's voice, trying to calm me. "Don't fight, Eponine."

He knew me? I turned around, saw the flower in the button-hole and the slicked dark hair. "Montparnasse."

He came closer. "Don't say it too loudly. I'm a wanted man . . ."

I'd have preferred a gendarme to him. I pushed his hand away. "For thieving and murdering?"

"You disapprove? I think you do: You've got piercing eyes, Eponine . . . And yet I know what you're doing here on the rue de Rivoli. Those letters in your pocket? You and your sister are trick-ing these well-dressed folk into parting with their pennies, aren't you? Which means you're no better than me . . ."

I resented this. "I *am* better than you! I've never murdered and I never would."

"Ah . . . I said the same thing once, but life is hard and people change. It becomes easier, Eponine. If they're very old, then what harm have you done? They'd have died soon anyway."

I wished he wasn't standing there. He was like a shadow with a musky smell, strong hands, and a knife in his belt. I felt tired suddenly. "Don't you wish for better?"

"Better? Of course. It's because I wish for better that I steal at all."

"You don't understand me, Montparnasse. I don't mean richer, I mean . . ." I paused. How could I explain it? "Don't you ever want to live a kinder life?"

I didn't think it was a hard question, but he flinched at it like it was an unknown bug, flying at him. "Kinder? What? Ha! How can *you* be a Thenardier? Do you know what your father would do if he heard such talk from his daughter's mouth?"

"Azelma is the better thief," I said quietly. "They say I'm too soft."

"I'm sure they're right. *Kindness* is a foolish word."

"That's what Maman says too."

I felt sour then. All these lanterns and carriages and soft rabbit fur and men with top hats and romance: Montparnasse was ruining all of it. All I wanted was to believe in *better*, just a bit. A little light and love and *hope*. I wanted to shake Montparnasse, to shout out that his heart might be missing but mine was still beating, and my conscience was beating too and I wouldn't let him make me feel hollow and useless and sad. How could he ever be happy, murdering? But I didn't do or say any of these things. I just whispered, "There are other ways to live."

"Other ways?"

"Moral ways. Other people survive without thieving, so why can't we?"

He laughed so loudly that people looked over. "Moral? Look around you, Eponine! How much morality do you see here? This lot have got their wealth from beating their servants and from their wicked business deals—and most won't give a single sou to the poor, I promise you that. See the shopkeepers? They'll take any coin they can, selling meat that's flyblown or fruit that's bruised—they don't care! As for the priests, they talk about helping the poor but have you seen the wealth they've got in their churches? The silver and gold?" He tutted, shook his head. "If you think this is a good world, you're mistaken. Being kind won't make a single bit of difference. It'll only make you poorer still."

I felt like telling him he was so wrong: that there *were* good people in the world and their goodness could fill a room. There *was* a better way—because I'd seen it in Montfermeil, all those years ago.

In a softer voice he said, "You believe in love too, I shouldn't wonder."

I felt like crying, then. "Yes," I answered. "I believe in it."

His smile was like a cat's smile to a mouse. "Love? It's a myth. But there's money in it. You're not ugly, Eponine: You could sell a kiss or two . . ."

My eyes brimmed with tears. I was done with him.

I ran away, over the river, and on toward Salpêtrière. I cried as I went. *I can't steal. I can't find a job. I can't find love or be beautiful. There's no point in anything.*

I ran all the way home and slipped on ice. My hands and knees were bleeding.

I'd never felt so hopeless or alone. Who could have imagined that this would be the moment?

I pushed open the door. I ran up the stairs without looking and I ran straight into someone. A boy. No one I knew.

He was walking down the stairs as I was running up them. He held my shoulders gently to stop me crashing into him, and looked right into my eyes.

"*Excusez-moi*, Mademoiselle."

ROOM FOUR

His hair was thick and dark and he was brown-eyed like me but his were darker, a sort of golden brown. They had little flecks in them as if sunshine had been stirred in. Freckles on his nose. A dimple in his left cheek as he smiled at me.

He didn't belong in the Gorbeau tenement at all, *at all*.

He let go of my shoulders. "You're crying," he said, frowning then. "Are you all right?"

I wasn't but I couldn't say so. I just nodded.

"Are you sure? I can't help you?"

I managed, "*Non*, Monsieur. *Merci*."

He gave a second smile, slipped past me, and made his way downstairs.

I stood very still. I just looked at the space where he'd been.

That night, I couldn't sleep. He couldn't live in the Gorbeau. *He must be a visitor.* I smiled at the stars through the window and thought, *Please let him visit again.*

*   *   *

In the morning, I went to Madame Bourgon. When she opened her door, she raised an eyebrow at me. "Ah. The elder Jondrette girl. What are you bothering me for?"

"Madame, I'm seeking a person who was here yesterday, a young gentleman. I think he's a visitor? He left a button and I've got to return it."

"A button?" She wasn't a fool. She knew that the Jondrettes would snatch a button and sell it, not give it back.

"Yes. A button. He was older than me—twenty, maybe? He wore a dark wool coat and his hair was a sort of chestnut color . . ."

Her mouth cracked into a gummy smile. "Aha! Him. I know the one . . . Pretty, isn't he? Four."

"Four?"

"Room Four."

"He visits the people who live in Room Four?"

She spat a brownish phlegm, wiped her mouth with her hand. "Visits? He doesn't visit. He rents Room Four."

"What?" I flinched. "He *lives* here? In the tenement?"

"You're surprised? You think he's too good for this place, do you? At least he pays on time, unlike your lot. Anyway, he's Room Four—I'm sure you could slide his button under his door . . ."

With that, she went.

Room Four? How long had he lived there? How come I hadn't seen him before? I couldn't believe it: the family called Jondrette lived in Room Five, next door.

I began to go back upstairs but then a thought struck me. I rushed back, knocked on Madame Bourgon's door a second time.

She was annoyed. "What now?"

"His name, Madame! Do you know his name?"

She sighed, fed up. "Marius. Marius Pontmercy."

I smiled as I left her. *It's a myth*, Montparnasse had said.

No, I thought. *It's real.* I knew that now.

MARIUS

I couldn't knock on his door—because what would I say? What would he think of my torn skirts and my knotted hair?

I'll wait, I thought. *I'll just wait and hope I might see him again.* But this was impossible to do: I was sent out to thieve every day. If I stayed behind, Maman would yell, "What are you doing? Get out! Find things! Shoo!" or Papa would raise his fist and call me *a lazy beast* . . . At night, even though I listened very hard for the sound of his key in the door of Room Four, I never did. There were too many other noises—barking dogs and crying babies and slamming doors. Papa's snores. Maman's curses about our poor thieving. I'd think, *I hope he can't hear her through the walls.*

Slowly, the dirtied snow melted away. In its place I saw the first small shoots of green. "My hands aren't numb anymore . . . ," said Azelma one day, amazed. She'd returned from her wanderings with coins and tobacco and a bottle of gin for Maman. "How nice it's *spring* now . . ."

February, then March. April came.

I just imagined him. He isn't real. Stupid Eponine . . .

But I knew he was real. Every time I went up or down stairs I'd practice what I might say to him—a little comment on the weather or a belated *Happy New Year*—and each time I heard someone else's footsteps I'd think, *This time . . .*

I did see him in the end, but it wasn't on the stairs.

It was early in the morning. Sun came through our grimy window so I dressed and crept out of the tenement before anyone else was awake. I found a water trough meant for horses. It was freshly filled and the water was clear, ungreened. I plunged my hands into it and washed myself—face, feet, between my legs and under my arms. I also washed my hair and threw it back so that it sent a spray of water out and a passing woman shouted, "Hey! Stop that! I'm soaked now!"

But it felt good to get the winter's dirt off me. I wandered back home wondering how long it would take for my hair to dry in the weak sunshine. For once I wasn't thinking about him.

Then, at the crossroads by the tenement, I looked up. My heart leapt. *It's him!* It had been months since I'd seen him, but I still recognized his coat and his thick hair, and I didn't care that my dress was sticking to me. *I'm going to follow him*, I thought. *I'll see where he goes and what he does . . .* I knew how I looked—scruffy, with scabs on my knees; I knew he wouldn't want to know me at all. But at least by watching him, I could get to know him.

He walked through the streets of Salpêtrière and I followed. My heart was racing but I was smiling too because I was happy just to see him again.

I made notes, in my head. *He is tall*—taller than me, but not so tall that he had to duck under doorways. *His shoulders are broad*— like he'd worked hard in his youth and still had the strength. *His skin is unlined.* I thought I heard him humming as he went.

He walked steadily, like he had a purpose. I thought maybe he was going to the rue de Rivoli, but he didn't go across the river. He walked east, away from the city. I'd never gone this way before and I saw that the street became earthy and some hedges appeared. It was a strange place, neither city nor countryside—it was called Austerlitz.

What's he doing out here?

We'd been walking for perhaps an hour when he stopped. I slipped into the shadow of a hazelnut tree.

There was a cottage. It was a small, ramshackle place and yet its garden was overgrowing with spring flowers. It had a pear tree and a lavender bush. There were flowers of such a deep, soft red that I wanted to reach out and touch them. Marius was smiling, looking at it all.

It had been ages since I'd seen a garden. I thought, *It's like Montfermeil with its wayside flowers.*

Then he opened the gate and walked through it, calling out, "Monsieur Mabeuf? Are you there?" I imagined him calling my name like that one day—*Eponine! Where are you?* I liked thinking it.

Marius came to this cottage a lot. On this first occasion, when my hair was still wet from the drinking trough, he stayed with the man called Mabeuf for an hour or more. Mabeuf was old—whiskery and hunched. His uncle? A relative? I didn't know. But they strolled slowly through the garden like friends, and I saw Mabeuf pointing at the flowers and the blossoms in his trees. Later they shook hands and I followed Marius home.

Now I knew he woke early, I began to do the same. While Maman and Papa and Azelma were still snoring, I crept out to follow him . . . And I was a fine follower. After all, I knew how to be quiet and stealthy. I could creep like a mouse so he'd never know I was there.

Once he bought a flask of milk from the dairy on rue Moustaffe and took it to Austerlitz as a gift. Another time, I moved the branches of the hazelnut tree aside and watched them sitting in the sunshine side by side, looking happy. And no matter what the weather was, they always trod around the garden. Marius would smell the dark red flowers or touch the lavender.

He didn't even really know I existed, and yet I already knew what his footsteps sounded like and what his shadow looked like as it passed beneath our door, and I knew how he tilted his head up when he looked at something beautiful—a flying bird or the French flag blowing in the wind. I followed him into the city sometimes, and if he stopped to listen to a speaker in the crowd— fiery talk of God, or the king, or a brave soul who cried, "Get rid of the guillotine! It is bloody and unjust!"—I'd watch him. He bit his bottom lip when he was thinking. A little crease appeared between his eyes.

I learned that he liked Les Halles with its vendors crying out, "Monsieur, Monsieur! Fresh figs from Toulouse! Or, "Honey from Avignon! Monsieur!" It was here that I saw a lady spill her figs to the floor. Marius knelt and helped her, picking them up one by one.

He's kind. He listens to people, and he thinks about things.

I liked everything I learned about him.

One day, he made his way along the rue de la Chanvrerie. It led to the place Saint-Michel. I gasped because he knew the Café Musain! Of all the cafés in Paris he chose this one, the one where I'd pressed my nose against the glass in the winter months. That man with the blond curls and those men who'd raised their glasses in a toast—*To Lamarque! Vive la république!*—must've been his friends because they cheered as he entered the café. Through the window I saw him in there, drinking. His cheeks were flushed with warmth.

My list grew longer and longer.

He's got nice friends. He looks up at cathedrals as he walks past them. People cheer when he walks into a room. He's kind to an old man in Austerlitz. When he passes a stray dog, he always pats it. He's got dimples. When he's very tired, he rubs his knuckles into the corners of his eyes.

If I were his, I'd take his hands and say, *Rest. I'll take care of you.*

Spring turned into summer. Paris had never looked more beautiful. I thought, *Speak to him, Eponine.* So I was brave, and I did.

THE VISIT

There were changes in me.

I didn't know, but Maman saw them first. I'd come back from a day's walking with a smile, or I'd be singing, and this puzzled her.

"Why are you singing? Stop it, it's annoying." She saw me brushing the knots out of my hair with a thistle head and said, "Vain, Eponine . . . ? You've not been that before."

Maman noticed too that I was stealing less than I ever had. One day she looked up from her sewing and said, "You're bringing back nothing these days—nothing! What's wrong with you? Are you actually *giving* those letters to people? Those letters that Papa wrote so well?"

I shrugged. I didn't want to lie.

"Well, do it! For heaven's sake! Azelma's stealing well, so why can't you? The weather might be warmer, but we still need to eat!" Maman returned to her sewing, tugged the needle fiercely. "You seem . . . distracted. And I don't like it, Eponine. Do you hear?"

Azelma was always stealing well. She returned with her pockets jangling, and our parents rubbed their hands and kissed her. She came back with all sorts of food—a haunch of goat or a basket of eggs. In late summer she rushed home and untied her bodice and skirts in the middle of the room and dozens of plums fell down around her.

"See! I can steal anything!" She laughed. "The grocer didn't even notice!"

That night, with all the plums around us, I said, "We've enough fruit to feed the whole of the Gorbeau if we want to . . ."

"Which we don't," snapped Papa. "Why would we want to share what's ours? With that wheezy couple in Room Seven or that sour old churchgoing cripple who talks to himself, in Room Nine?"

"Or," said Maman, "that snooty, well-dressed boy next door, in Room Four? I won't share a *thing* with him. I bet he's got money hidden away."

Azelma swallowed. "Really? Then maybe we should give him one of Papa's letters? Let's trick him too."

Maman grinned, her mouth full of plums. "A wonderful idea! Do it now, Azelma! Have you got a letter?"

I spoke up. "Room Four? Let me, Maman."

She flinched. "You? Miss Goody-Two-Shoes?"

I nodded. My stomach felt hard and my hands shook, but I said, "Yes, I'll go. It's my turn, after all."

Papa spat out a plum stone. "Don't mess it up—do you hear?"

* * *

I went to the corner. I rinsed my face and washed my hands.

I can do this. I can speak to him.

I trembled. I didn't want to trick him but at least I had a reason to speak to him now. My insides turned over and over.

I picked up one of Papa's letters.

I went out into the corridor and stood in front of his door. The number 4 looked back at me. I smoothed my hair and cleared my throat.

Take a deep breath, I told myself. *Be brave.*

I knocked three times: *bang-bang-bang.*

His voice! It called out, "Come in, Madame Bourgon!"

I opened the door. "It isn't Madame Bourgon, Monsieur."

There he was—sitting at a writing desk. He wore a dark blue shirt and woolen breeches, and his feet were in socks, without shoes. There were shadows under his eyes like he hadn't been sleeping. He wore the slight crease between his eyes that I knew. "*Oui*, Mademoiselle?"

"Excuse me, Monsieur. I live next door, in Room Five. We met once—on the stairs? I ran into you, and . . ." I paused. Of course he didn't remember but I couldn't help feeling crushed. "I've got a letter for you."

I held it out. He kept looking at my face for a moment, and then he reached for the note. "I remember. Back in the winter? You were upset, I think. Even though you said you were all right."

He did remember!

I nodded.

"Had someone hurt you?"

"Only with words."

He gave a small smile. "Sometimes words can be the most hurtful things of all." He opened the letter and started to read.

His room was much better than ours. It was the same size, with a hearth in it, but he also had a bed with a proper coverlet and a desk with a matching chair, and a mirror in a fine frame. What was the frame worth? (I'd been raised to ask such things.) And there was a piece of material at the window—a curtain. I'd not seen curtains since we'd left Montfermeil.

There was a bookcase too. Without thinking, I went to it. It had been years since I'd held or read a book. I pulled one off the shelf. "Books! You have books!"

He looked up, surprised. "You read?"

"I used to. I know I don't look much—all rags and bones—but I learned to read when I was very small and I loved it. I read about Paris, and those books made me want to come here. Sometimes I'd read to my little brother . . ." I paused. In a quieter voice I said, "It's been a long time since I read a book."

What else could I tell him? I said, "I like walking too. I've walked and walked through Paris and seen so much . . ." I couldn't stop suddenly, found myself babbling all my secrets, as if now that I'd started talking I might never stop. "And how white Notre-Dame looks at night and the grassy slopes of Champ de Mars, and the boulevards. I've peeped into theaters! And I'd love to see a proper play, like ladies do. Maybe one day. Paris is so beautiful, Monsieur! Before I came here, I used to sleep in ditches or under an upturned boat—yes, I know how that sounds! But it wasn't so bad. We could swim, and catch fish there . . . I think there is beauty in most things, if you look for it, don't you? Even the dirtiest things can be lovely, underneath. I knew a man who said that the speckled peaches were the sweetest of all, and I like that. There can be light in dark places—don't you think, Monsieur Marius?"

I'd said too much. But it was hard to be calm, and my head and heart were racing.

He stared at me. He looked amused and puzzled. "You know my name?"

I blushed. "*Oui.* I heard . . . Madame Bourgon say it . . ." It was the truth.

"Then I should know yours. It would be fair, wouldn't it?"

I smiled. "Eponine."

"Eponine?"

"I was named after a heroine in one of Maman's books."

"*C'est un joli nom.* And it sounds like you've had an interesting life, Eponine. Sleeping under boats?"

I wasn't sure how to answer that.

Marius lifted the letter. "Did you write this?"

I winced. The letter . . . "It's not my work . . . it's my father's. Please forgive me for giving it to you. It's full of lies and I didn't want to give it to you but I've got no real choice in it. My mother's crippled. My father is . . . well, he ordered me to give you this and I can't disobey him. We're penniless, you see."

"Many are." He looked out the window. "If the souls who died forty years ago in that revolution could see us now . . ." Then he looked back to me. "Aren't there better ways of trying to get a sou or two?"

I felt so ashamed. All my talk of books and beauty suddenly seemed very foolish; *I'm a grubby thief, that's all.* "There are. And I do try. But it's hard to get a job when you're someone like me."

He folded the letter and handed it back. "Well, you've been honest enough in explaining the note to me. And, Eponine, I know how poor you are. I've seen your family on the stairs and I've caught your sister dipping her hands in my coat pocket . . ." He opened a drawer in his desk and offered me a five-franc coin.

I gasped. Five francs? That was more money than I'd stolen in months and months. My parents would be so happy if I handed it to them—but I shook my head. "I can't take that. It feels wrong."

"Why? You aren't stealing it. I'm offering it willingly."

I suddenly felt very sad. I didn't want his pity; I wanted something else. Pity was the last thing I wanted. "But, Monsieur, it's your money."

"And so I can choose to spend it how I like. Take it. You need it more than I do. Have you seen how thin you are, how unwell you look?"

My shame was greater than ever then. The word *unwell* meant *ugly*. *Thin* meant *boyish*, and not like a girl at all. In all my dreams, he'd told me I was beautiful—but those were just stupid dreams.

I could barely speak to him. I reached for the coin.

"Buy food with it."

"Thank you," I murmured. And I hurried from his room with tears in my eyes.

* * *

The others cooed over the five francs. Maman stroked me and smiled.

"He must be a proper fool, that boy," said Papa. "Good to know."

But I thought, *No, he isn't a fool! He wasn't tricked, he was kind, that's all.* And I comforted myself by thinking that a little food and summer sun might make me look much better, and maybe he'd meet me out in the street and say, *Goodness, how you've changed, Eponine! You don't look unwell anymore.* I looked back at each word he'd said to me. *C'est un joli nom*—did that have meaning in it?

I stared at the wall between us that night. I imagined what he might be doing at that moment—sitting at his desk, or drawing the curtain, or taking off his shoes and lying down on that coverlet. Might he be looking at his books, thinking, *Eponine has touched these . . . ?* Briefly I pretended; it was a nice daydream to have. But I knew the truth: I looked *thin* and *unwell*, with bruises and hollow cheeks. Of course he wasn't thinking of me.

A WALK AT SUNSET

The five francs lasted a while. It bought meat, cheese, a new darning needle, and tobacco for Papa's pipe. It bought me freedom too because I could follow Marius without having to give out letters, or steal.

June bloomed all around us. In Montfermeil this had been the month of hawthorn blossom and the early roses climbing over the churchyard wall. In Paris, there were fewer flowers—just some weeds in the rue des Gobelins and roses in gents' buttonholes. But it was enough.

That was a hot June too. Maman fanned herself in our room, saying, "There's no air . . . and the smell! What's that horrible smell?"

The heat meant that everything—rubbish, milk, human muck, the offal by the butchers' doors—rotted far more quickly. A stench seemed to rise from the river as well. Some people walked with handkerchiefs held over their noses, or with posies in their hand.

Marius was the one good thing in my life. I wanted to talk to him again. I'd left Room Four feeling tearful and ashamed, but as the days passed, I could only think of the best parts of my time with him—his concern for me (*Had someone hurt you?*) and how quickly he had forgiven me for the note. One hot day, I followed him again. In the summer heat, he moved more slowly; he moved from the shade of a house to the shade of a church, or he'd pause beneath a bridge for a while. He carried a bag with him—books, I suspected. An inkwell and quill?

I followed him to the Café Musain in the place Saint-Michel, where he sat outside with his friends. They read his books and papers, drank and wrote and talked beneath the shade of a tree.

I nestled against the stones of a nearby church, the one with the clock that chimed on the hour, and watched how he drank and how he moved his hand through his hair. They talked with gestures and loud voices. I recognized some of his friends: the boy with half-moon spectacles who shouted through cupped hands. And the boy with golden curls who stood, thumped the table, and said, "Yes! That's it!" Their passion hadn't changed.

I watched for a long time. In the end, my legs cramped so I stood and turned to go. But then I heard my name called out: "Eponine?"

I felt my heart leap.

"Eponine, is that you?" Marius was walking toward me. He'd risen from his chair, put his bag across his shoulder, and was making his way across the square. "I thought it was you! What are you doing all the way out here? You're a long way from the Gorbeau."

I couldn't say, *Following you.* I could barely speak at all. I just shrugged and tried to look like my heart wasn't beating faster and my hands weren't shaking. "Just . . . walking. You know I like walking."

"Ah." He smiled. "Of course. Walking all round Paris. Well, I'm heading back home now; would you walk with me? For a while, at least?"

So we began to walk through the streets, Marius and me. We walked slowly, side by side, moving around the dirt in the streets and stepping over potholes. In my head, I told myself, *Speak to him. Ask him things.*

"Are you often at the Café Musain, Monsieur Marius?"

He smiled. "We're neighbors, aren't we? Just call me Marius— or else I will need to call you Mademoiselle Eponine, which all sounds a bit too formal, don't you think?"

I blushed.

"Yes, I go there often," he went on. "My friends meet there— friends from my student days. They are . . ." He considered which word to use. "Fiery. Full of ideas and passion. Patriotic, of course."

"Are you?"

"Patriotic? Yes, I am. France deserves far better than all this fighting and disease and unfairness . . . Its people deserve more."

"You support the man called Lamarque?"

He looked across at me, wide-eyed. "I do! You do too?"

I didn't want to lie to him. "To be honest, I don't know too much about politics and kings . . . I've just heard people talking of

Larmarque, that's all. I've never been to school. I'm not sure I'm very clever."

He laughed. "Oh, I don't believe that! You read books, don't you? You were so taken with my bookcase, I remember. There are people who've been to university who aren't readers of books *at all*, Eponine—people who say they're clever and well-read but in fact they're not: They're just rich! Don't assume you're worth less than them. I imagine you're smarter than most."

I smiled. *He thinks I'm smart.*

We walked across the Seine. We paused on the bridge, looked at the sunlight on the water and how the sky was turning gold and pink.

"And your life, until now? Tell me about it. It sounds like a curious thing."

It *had* been curious, I supposed. "Perhaps. We left our town six years ago. We were . . ."—should I tell him? Yes, I decided. I would always speak truthfully to him—"running from the law. My father committed a crime. So we hid."

"For six years?" He seemed amazed.

"Yes. It was hard, that's true. But I got to see some beautiful things—like full moons and frosty mornings . . ." Briefly, I thought of Gavroche. I shrugged. "It could have been worse."

"And it could have been better too, I think. You're generous with your words."

Generous? I'd never been called that before. *Smart and generous.* I beamed. "And you? Your life?"

He looked down at the river. "What can I tell you? My parents have died. No brothers or sisters. I see my friends as my family and I love them just as much. I love my country too. I love Paris."

He loves them. He seemed to love so much—and what did I love? I wasn't sure that I had any friends. And I didn't know Paris as well as he did.

As we left the bridge and wandered on, I said, "Marius? May I ask . . . ?"

He smiled, turned his head.

"What are your dreams?" It was a big question, I knew that, but he didn't seem to mind.

"My dreams?"

"Yes. What you imagine when you're alone. What you hope for, in the future?"

He kept his smile but it looked a little sadder. "I'm not sure I've been asked this before." He thought awhile. "I want France to be a republic, of course. No more kings and queens . . ."

"But for yourself?"

He seemed bashful, suddenly. "It doesn't suit a man to talk of love, not unless he's a poet or an artist and can afford to have such dreams. But I was a lonely child and . . . well, I think I'd like a family of my own, one day. A wife to love." He smiled. "Who knows?"

"I'd like that too. A person to love."

"You don't have that now?"

I couldn't speak for a while. The sun was low, and I could feel myself trembling inside. Were we really talking like this? Him and me?

He pointed out the tiny things I had never seen before—how doves perched on the stonework of Notre-Dame and the urchins playing in the fountains near Les Invalides. It made me think of Gavroche again, but they were all too old to be him. Poor Gavroche. "See the light now, Eponine? How it's catching the sides of the houses . . ."

It was gold and orange. I nodded: This was *his* Paris. It was real—not perfect like in romance novels. I knew that he saw the begging and dirt, the drunks and the thin, scavenging dogs, and I knew that he longed for it to end—"When Lamarque makes us a republic again . . . ," he said. But then he pointed out a single weed growing through a cracked wall, like he was a bird, high up. "See that?"

"Yes."

"It's a beautiful thing too, don't you think?"

"Yes." And I did. Everything was.

He took my hand very briefly to help me over a ditch and I thought, *He's holding my hand . . . and we fit perfectly.*

I wanted the walk to last forever but, too soon, the Gorbeau stood before us.

"Eponine," he said, "thank you for your company. I've enjoyed it."

"Me too."

His face was glowing from a day in the sun. His lashes were so long that they seemed to brush his cheekbones when he looked down to find his key. He was a boy who loved his friends and sunlight and France and the sound of urchins playing and he wanted love, just like I did.

"Good-night," he said, and opened his door.

After he'd gone, I looked at the number 4 and knew it was all too late now: I loved him. I could feel it inside me.

"Good-night," I whispered.

Generous and *smart* . . .

He hadn't called me *beautiful* but it didn't matter: I'd felt it, in his company. He'd made me feel beautiful and interesting for the first time in my life.

THE ROSE AMONG
THE ROSES

I wanted to walk with him all the time. But also, I didn't want him to see too much of me and get bored, or to think with a sigh, *There she is again* . . . I wanted to be a surprise to him. A chance meeting. A happy coincidence that made him say, *Ah! It's good to see you again!*

I told myself, *Be casual, Eponine. Don't let yourself be seen for a while.*

Give him a chance to miss you.

I busied myself elsewhere for three whole weeks. I tried my hardest. But in the end, I couldn't stay away. One bright July day I saw him walking southwest, away from the Seine. Not the Café Musain? So where?

I followed him farther into the quarter called Saint-Germain. This was where the university was, and there were lots of cafés and bars here too. There was a fiddler busking on a street corner and I saw Marius pause and give him a coin. He said, "You play very well."

He kept walking. He crossed the boulevard Saint-Germain and turned left. Ahead of us there were tall iron gates, wide open, and beyond them I could see more greenery than I'd seen in eight months of living in Paris. The grassy lawn was huge. The trees were emerald green. Flower beds were like rainbows with all the colors in them.

Marius walked through those gates and into the garden.

I stopped a passerby. "Monsieur? *Excusez-moi?* What's this place called?"

He answered as if I was an idiot. "Why, these are Les Jardins du Luxembourg!" He walked away, shaking his head.

Les Jardins du Luxembourg! I'd heard of them. They were the elegant gardens that surrounded Le Palais du Luxembourg itself and it was here that ladies strolled with their tiny dogs, where men walked with their pipes and smart conversations. *Paris's garden*, I thought. Wouldn't it be a lovely place to bump into him? To spend a little time?

I smoothed my hair and hurried after him, into the garden. Inside, it was even more beautiful—with the Palais' golden columns and its fountains sparkling in the sun, and the shady promenades beneath the line of trees . . . It suited him.

Marius sat down on a wooden bench, partly shaded. I sat down on another bench a little distance from him. He took a book from his pocket, crossed his left leg over his right leg, and started to read.

He looked so peaceful that I couldn't go to him. I just watched him. I wondered what I might say to him, how to start a conversation—and I imagined his answers, in my head. Only when the shadows lengthened did he stand up and fold his book away. He walked quickly as if following somebody, like I was following him. But out on the boulevard Saint-Germain, he looked from left to right and scratched his head. Whoever he'd been following was gone.

He started to go there every day. He chose the same bench in the sunshine and always carried a book. I also saw that he always wore the same clothes—a suit with a cravat and polished shoes. They seemed a strange choice for hot weather but he looked handsome in them.

I will speak to him today, I thought. I thought this most days.

But one day I told myself, *Today is the day*. I'd brushed my hair and washed my clothes, and I'd eaten mint to sweeten my breath: I was ready to walk by his side, again. I found I couldn't sit on the bench where I normally did because an old man was sleeping on it, hat tipped over his face, so I found another. This one was beside a rose bush. Its roses were deeply perfumed—such a sweet smell among the city's stench. The flowers half hid me so I had to move them to see Marius's face.

From this new angle I could see that his eyes weren't on the pages at all. Had they ever been? He was just pretending to read, because his eyes were actually looking toward an avenue of trees.

I didn't understand. What was he looking at? I followed his gaze.

Two people were sitting on a bench, as he was. One was a man with graying hair and a soft, kind face (no yellow coat; the yellow coat was gone) and the other was a girl with sunshine-colored hair.

HIS LOVE

Everyone has daydreams. I've had plenty of them. I used to dream of finding a Louis d'or coin on the ground or of my mother throwing me up in the air with delight, crying out, *Eponine!* Later, I had daydreams of a prince passing by on a white horse: he'd point at me and say *her* and I'd be plucked from my life and into a better one.

Then there was Marius—and all these daydreams fell away.

After our sunset walk through Paris, I had just four daydreams in the world and I handled them like jewels.

In the first, Marius was sitting on his bench in Les Jardins du Luxembourg. He turned and said, "Will you join me, Eponine?" and I nodded and sat beside him. From there, he told me all about the world—politics, travel, art, love. We smiled at each other and like this, we passed the day.

In my second daydream, he was walking. His face struck up like a match on seeing me: "Eponine! Why! I was thinking about you at that very moment . . ." He came to me, took my hands and kissed them and said, "I must tell you—oh, I *must* tell you—the truth is, I'm lost without you. Since we walked back from the Café Musain together, I cannot sleep or eat . . ."

In my third daydream, it wasn't a book in his lap. It was a notebook and he was writing poetry in it: *I know what true beauty is; it's Eponine.* He thought this, despite my torn dress and muddy feet.

But my fourth daydream was my favorite. It was a wordless dream: He didn't speak in it and I didn't either. He simply found me in Les Jardins, touched my cheek very lightly. Were we by the fountains? Sometimes. Or in those half-lit avenues. Then he held me as gently and his nose would touch my nose and like this I felt safe and loved.

Those were my four daydreams. Over and over, I cradled them.

But they died as I moved those roses aside. They died when I saw Marius's face—filled with love? Desire? Wonder?—looking at another girl's face.

Look. Oh no, no, no . . .

I stumbled away from my bench and onto my knees, my hands to my mouth. Cosette? Could it really be her? She wasn't wearing a sackcloth anymore, just as I thought she would not. Instead, she wore a floral-printed frock with a cream lace trim and a bonnet with a satin bow. She sat so neatly—with her hands in her lap and her ankles pressed together—that I almost didn't recognize her. But I did; I knew it was her.

There was no doubt. The girl who'd slept in cobwebs. The girl who'd scrubbed every floor—*left right, left right*—on her knees.

Euphrasie. But Maman calls me Cosette.

The gentleman was Jean Valjean. Age had grayed his hair at the sides and he seemed wider in the chest—but he still had the same kind face I remembered. He was glancing at what she held.

A book, like Marius. And like Marius, she was only pretending to read it. Her eyes were fixed on his.

I brought my hands away from my mouth. *They are staring at each other.* They were. I looked down at the ground where I was kneeling, at the stones and rose petals, but all I could think of was their faces. How they'd smiled at each other, across the flower beds.

Eight years since I had seen her.

I felt lots of things: grief, sorrow, jealousy. I felt stupid for thinking he could ever love me too because what was I? *Stupid, for having washed your face, and eaten mint, and felt hopeful . . .* I felt shocked as well, as if I'd dropped a wondrous thing—glass-made and dazzling—and it'd broken into a million pieces so that I had nothing left at all.

This too: I felt angry. It rose up like a river and it flooded everything.

That brat and the boy I loved.

It isn't fair, it isn't fair. I've tried to be good. I've looked for beauty in all things and I've been kind when I can be and I've only ever stolen because I was ordered to . . . I've prayed for little Gavroche. I've picked peaches for a crippled man and I've been thankful for the tiny things—like the stars and birdsong and a warm chestnut . . .

She has everything! She's got beauty and grace and nice clothes and a father who loves her! It's not fair that she has Marius too.

I marched from Les Jardins. I kicked a stone. I muttered, "What's the point?" And I remembered my mother's words from many years ago: *Then be cruel! Cruel! It's what will save you.*

I was so angry. And sad and jealous and lonely. I'd wanted him to like me. I'd wanted his sunshine after years of cold and dark. The pebble in my heart was back, and it went knock . . . knock . . . knock . . . louder and stronger than ever.

And I wasn't the only angry person in Paris. *Everyone is fed up of their poverty and rumbling bellies while the king eats veal with silver knives and forks. Everyone is tired of feeling hopeless and grubby and cold, like me.* We all wanted to rise up in anger. Fight. Kill.

I ran up the stairs of the Gorbeau thinking, *I'll be cruel again. I'll hiss and spit at her and I'll make her sorry for having a pretty face . . .*

I would not be kind anymore. I would be a true Thenardier like I promised I'd be, long ago.

THE PLAN

I flung open the door. My parents looked up. Maman was using a stone to crush a bone for its marrow and Papa was smoking his pipe.

"Eponine? What've you got? Money or jewels?"

"Better than that. I've found a rich man."

"What? Where?"

"In the Jardins du Luxembourg."

Maman dropped the stone, hobbled forward. "How do you know he's rich? Is he dressed smartly? Well spoken?"

"No, not smartly. And I haven't heard his voice."

"Then how do you know? He might be quite poor!"

I shook my head. He had money, I was sure: How else could he dress Cosette in such fine clothes? Nor had I forgotten the Louis d'or that he'd placed in a wooden shoe, eight years before. "I'm certain he's rich. He's careful with his money, that's all. But he'll give to a worthy cause, I reckon—like a starving child . . ."

My father gave his foxy smile. "I like this . . . You're sure? He'll give?"

"As sure as I can be. I think we should give him one of Papa's letters. We should give him the very best letter that Papa has ever written!"

"In Les Jardins du Luxembourg, you say?"

"Yes. I could give him the letter and trick him." I felt vengeful, on fire. "We must get every penny from him!"

Papa began to write the note. He was careful: He wanted the perfect letter. He began to write it and then, irritated, threw the paper in the fire. He started a second time and then roared with frustration, "This is rubbish! I've got to write something subtle . . . clever. This letter must be just right!"

I watched him. I sat by the window, chewing my fingernails.

After several days he said, "What's his name? This man? Do you know?"

I nearly said, *Yes, Papa—it is Jean Valjean.* But something stopped me and I kept the secret inside. Papa would, surely, recognize the name. He'd pause and narrow his eyes and say, *Didn't we meet him once . . . Didn't he buy that wretched Cosette? For far too small a sum? Ha! That nasty do-good of a man . . .* They hated him and they might do more than trick him with letters, if they knew who he was. Papa still had that bone-handled knife.

This is my consolation: I thought of tricking him with the letter, but that was all. I didn't want to hurt him or Cosette and so I never said their names.

I was heartbroken. But I never wanted their deaths.

EPONINE WISHES

He loves her. I looked at my reflection in shop windows or the passing glass of carriages. I thought, *Why her, not me?* But I knew why.

I'd always known she was beautiful. I was four years old when we met, and even then her hair was gold and shiny. She wore sackcloth and she scrubbed the grease from the walls yet I watched her and thought, *I wish I looked like you.*

What part of Cosette had made the people in Montfermeil whisper *Poor dove* when they saw her, or *Such a pretty thing . . .* before moving on with their own small lives? She was neat. She had elegance so that even when she swept the yard, she did so very daintily. Her hair curled at the ends. Her lips were rose-colored. Her eyes were like pools—blue, deep, reflecting the trees and the sky.

In Les Jardins, she looked exactly the same. She was older but she was still Cosette. I stood on the rue Christine. It was evening. I could see my reflection in the candlemaker's window. *Of course he loves her, not me*, I thought—for the girl who looked back at me was drab and bruised and impossibly thin. All the thistles in the world had not made her hair tidy; knots still hung on it with feathers and twigs. Her collarbone stuck out. Her forehead was lined. She didn't have either a waist or a chest to speak of. Her lips were cracked and dry.

Of course he'd choose Cosette. It would be like choosing between a puddle and the sea. A snapped stick and a springtime tree. A pebble and a mountain.

I was so silly to think he'd love me. Silly to think he liked walking beside me, that day.

I stole again. I returned to being the Eponine from the Sergeant of Waterloo who plucked rings off fingers, snapped buckles off shoes. I did no good deeds. I only thought, *Why bother?* It didn't seem worth it anymore.

I walked home with sous in my pockets. A wind blew and the few, thin trees were turning brown.

Autumn was coming. My hopes for a better life—for a kind and loving one—were blown away with the leaves.

THE LETTER IS DELIVERED

It took several weeks. Then at the start of October I woke to find Papa standing over me, holding the letter. "Done," he said. "My best letter yet! Your turn now."

It began:

Monsieur,

Forgive me for writing to you, and for troubling you in such a way. I write humbly, and if any inconvenience or discomfort should occur as a result of this letter, then I apologize sincerely and on my knees . . .

I looked up at him, amazed. This didn't sound like Papa at all.

He cracked his knuckles, smiling. "Impressed? Well, I thought I should be polite. He's a gentleman, you say?"

I read the rest of the letter. In it, he'd written:

We are dying, Monsieur, my children are. We have our wits but wits cannot always feed us. Others may steal, in these dark times, but we are good, religious folk and wouldn't steal a feather from a passing bird. All we can do is ask for help from other godly souls like you, Monsieur . . .

"Take it to him. Cough. Say you are ill. Look thinner than that."

"Look thinner?" How could I make myself look thinner?

"Dirty your face!" called Maman. "Use ash from the fire! Let's find horse dung in the street, and . . ."

They tried these things. They smeared my face and clothing until Papa nodded. "Better. But still . . . it isn't quite enough. A cough and a dirty face are good but we need more." He thought for a moment. Then he raised his hand. I looked up at it and wondered why it was there. Then he hit me. His fist met my cheek and I fell against the fireplace. The pain was quick and hot.

"Luc!" Maman squawked. "What did you strike the girl for? She's been stealing well for us lately!"

I felt a warm trickle coming from my nose. It pooled on my top lip and I tasted blood.

"To mark her, you stupid woman! She's got to look as poor and needy as we can make her. A swelling will rise up now. She can say she was robbed in the street or that she was injured whilst defending a poorer soul than herself, or perhaps she struggled against a man who wished her to enter into dark dealings, and her noble heart refused to . . . It'll get his pity, you see?"

I caught my nosebleed in cupped hands. My cheek began to swell up, closing my right eye so I could hardly see.

Papa was triumphant. "See? See how awful she looks?"

Maman mopped my bloodied hands with her skirt. "Stop whimpering, child. Your father's right; this is a good plan. We'll leave some blood on your face because it does make you look more pitiful. Now, deliver your letter. Go!"

Autumn's smell was in the air—woodsmoke, leaves. I stumbled toward Les Jardins du Luxembourg past the old tannery, the quarries, and the pits. Past the graveyard.

I made it to boulevard Saint-Germain. I didn't care that people were staring at my bleeding face. For nearly a month, all I'd thought of was him and her. Marius and Cosette.

Les Jardins du Luxembourg looked different—the trees were coppery and the flowers were mostly gone. It was nearly a month since I'd been there; what if they didn't come here anymore, if it was too cold to read their books in the open air? His bench was empty. No Marius.

I blinked painfully. What of Cosette and Jean Valjean?

There. There they were, but they weren't sitting. Instead they were walking arm in arm, scuffing through the fallen leaves. She wore a coat trimmed with fox fur and his muffler was high around his neck.

I didn't have a scarf of my own. Instead, I half hid my face with my waist-long hair. Eight years had passed but I didn't want to risk them recognizing me.

Briefly, I felt very guilty. But then I remembered, *He loves her, not you. Cosette, who has everything,* and it made me walk toward them.

"Monsieur? *Un moment, s'il vous plaît?*"

They turned.

I felt like I was standing in the tavern in Montfermeil again. Was it Christmas Eve? Was I a child, playing with the cat?

"Mademoiselle? Can I help?" He saw the threadbare clothes and the peeling skin and the dirt. He stared through my hair at my swollen eye and bloodied nose. His gaze seemed kinder than it had ever been.

Cosette gasped—a dainty, feminine gasp. "Papa! Her face! The poor creature . . ."

I thought, *Be cruel. Be cruel, Eponine.*

I held the letter out. "Would you read this, Monsieur? I feel ashamed to have to trouble you and your daughter in this way— and please, shoo me away if I offend you with my rag and tatters. Others do; I'm used to it. Only, please know that we are very desperate and I choose you because you have a kindly face . . ."

He read the letter. Cosette read it too, leaning on his upper arm. She murmured, *"Mon Dieu,"* very sadly. Then Valjean folded the letter. He looked at me, shifted his jaw from side to side.

"Dying, you say?"

"Yes, sir. My sister is so thin—far thinner than I am. She can't have long to live."

"And the injury? To your face? That looks freshly done."

"Defending her, Monsieur. She was set upon by some terrible men and I fought them because she is too weak to fight herself."

He stood very still as he listened.

"Forgive me for showing this note to you. If you're unable to assist, then I will only thank you for your time and move elsewhere. We have no choice, you see . . ."

"And where do you live, precisely?"

I flinched. *Where do we live?* I didn't think he'd ask this. "The Gorbeau tenement."

"Is it far?"

"In Salpêtrière. The long, dark building that faces the beginning of the rue des Gobelins."

"Near the tannery?"

"Yes, near there."

"I know of it. I'll come to you shortly."

I was shocked. "What? You'll come? To the Gorbeau?"

"Yes, I will—because I wish to see your poverty myself. I wish to see your poor, malnourished sister so that I can understand how best to help her. Money alone might not be enough. Tell your family to expect me. I shall be with you by the evening."

I wasn't sure what to say. He'd come to the Gorbeau? What would my parents say? He was meant to simply give me some coins—a franc or two—here, in Les Jardins.

I stuttered. "I-I'll tell them. Thank you."

He did give me a coin—a franc. "That is for you. On your way home, stop in the market or on a street corner and find a little food for yourself because no creature can stay as thin as you are."

I nodded and turned, and as I did, I heard Cosette say, "Oh, how can she bear it? The poor dear thing!"

*　　*　　*

I ran, thinking, *He's coming to Gorbeau!* But I also ran with an ache in my belly, deep down. It wasn't hunger: It was the ache I'd had when I heard of the bishop being stabbed and when I saw Babet's eye through the hole in the wall. It came when I felt unsafe and frightened.

Trouble is on its way. I was sure of it.

The streets grew dark and cold.

THE FIRE IS PUT OUT

I threw open the door.

"He's coming!"

Papa sprang from the chair. Maman and Azelma were both crouching by the fire, blowing on their hands.

"What? Who?"

"The rich man!"

"Coming here?" Papa's eyes flashed.

"Yes. I gave him the letter and he read it"—I was puffing—"and he said he'd come here to see how poor we are. To see how he could help us."

"By giving us money! That's how he can help us!" Maman spat into the fire. "Why the *hell* is he coming *here*?"

But Papa stroked his bristly chin. In a thoughtful voice he said, "When?"

"This evening, he said."

"On his own?"

"I think so. He's got a daughter but I don't think he'll bring her. He seems protective." *Like a papa should be*, I thought.

163

Papa started to smile. He paced the room, said, "Perfect . . . This is perfect! Let me think . . . Oh, yes! What a wonderful plan this is . . ."

"A plan?" Azelma didn't understand. None of us did.

"Give me that bucket." He seized it from Maman and threw water on the fire.

Maman screeched. "What the hell are you doing? That fire is the only heat we've got! It's bitter outside and they say sleet is coming—and how are we going to keep warm, now? Or cook? You stupid . . ."

Papa ignored her. He took the wooden chair and broke it. "The poorer we look, the better. Azelma? Break the windowpane."

"What?" She straightened. She tended to do as she was told but now she frowned at him. "Break it? But it's so cold, Papa! The fire is gone and if it starts to sleet as Maman says . . ."

"Don't talk back to me! Just break it!"

"Papa . . ."

"We want him to feel sorry for us, girl! We want him to think we're the most wretched and miserable creatures in Paris—cold and perishing and thin! So break that window! Do it!"

She crept to the window. She looked unsure. "How should I break it?"

"With your fist!"

I should've said *no*, because I knew that she'd hurt herself that way. But Azelma did it anyway. She punched the glass and two sounds followed: the tinkling of glass falling on the street below and Azelma screaming, "Oh! Oh! The blood! Oh, it hurts, Maman!"

A sharp wind rushed into the room.

Maman hobbled to Azelma, snapping at Papa, "Oh, well done, Luc! One daughter with a swollen face and the other with a bleeding arm! A fine job! Azelma, stop wailing."

"The worse they look the better! Don't you understand?" He reached for his coat, said, "Now I must tell the others . . ."

I looked up. "What others?"

"Ha! A rich man? Coming here? And all on his own . . . ? It's like a lamb coming to a butcher's shop, don't you think? With the others we'll be able to get every penny from him, every button, every silk thread . . . We'll tie him up if we have to! And if he tries to struggle . . . Well, Babet and Claquesous know a trick or two."

The Patron Minette. My heart turned to stone. I couldn't speak.

He went to the door and called back. "Azelma? When he comes, you've got to act like you're dying. Don't stanch the blood or clean yourself up. Josephine? Hide your stick and say you can't walk at all. And Eponine? You'll be our lookout. Stand beneath the dead white tree by the cemetery, and if you see a gendarme or any nosy soul, run back and tell us . . . Understand?"

He didn't wait for an answer. He just rubbed his hands and left the room, saying, "A fortune is coming, I can feel it!"

We listened to his footsteps as he hurried away.

A butcher's shop? A lamb? Oh, what have I done? I trembled. As Azelma stared at her bleeding arm and as Maman shivered by the damp hearth, I just thought of Montfermeil. I thought of the kitchen there. Rabbits slung on hooks. Plucked hens. Meat.

Whatever happened to the girl who'd tried to be kind? Who'd polished the church's brass knocker and lifted insects from the old nag's drinking trough?

I'd never felt worse than I did at that moment.

They're going to kill Valjean tonight.

BENEATH THE DEAD WHITE TREE

I found the dead white tree by the cemetery and pressed myself against its bark.

What can I do? How can I stop this?

I couldn't run to the gendarmerie because where might I find them? And they'd probably only get to the Gorbeau too late. I couldn't call out, *Help! Help!* because the Patron Minette would be lurking nearby now and might kill me to make me be quiet. All I could hope for was that Valjean might walk past me; I could warn him then.

It began to sleet. It came through the leafless branches and stung my swollen cheek. It made it hard to see but I keep watching the street in case Valjean should come. I imagined him—his scarf, his hat, the graying parts of his hair . . .

Don't come here, I'd tell him. *Stay away.*

The sleet grew worse and worse. In the cemetery, I heard noises—a twig snapping and the scuttle of a rat. *I'm alone in the cold and dark*, I thought. There weren't even any stars.

But I wasn't alone.

I smelled tobacco. Then I heard the slow, careful tread of boots on wet ground. A man's footsteps.

I stepped out from the tree. "Who's there?"

It was Montparnasse. He was completely in shadow but I knew it was him. I could smell the oil he put in his hair and see the red tip of his cigarette.

"Well, well . . ." He exhaled, blowing smoke above me. "Mademoiselle Eponine. What can you be doing on the corner of a cemetery, on such an unpleasant night?" He stepped forward so that I could see him better. "It'll be snowing," he went on, "before long. I'd sooner find a fireside . . . Wouldn't you?"

I said nothing.

"I'm confused, Mademoiselle . . . you see, this is the hour for dark deeds, I think? For theft and trickery? No honest person would be out in this weather and so late . . . But you? A thief? Surely not. Because the last time we met, on the rue de Rivoli, you told me that you believed in love . . ."

He was mocking me. "You know why I'm here," I muttered.

"Yes, I do. A rich horse is being unsaddled in Salpêtrière tonight . . . Babet told me."

"Babet is close by?"

"Oh, yes. He's hiding in the shadows too. They're waiting for their moment to sneak into the Gorbeau."

"You'll sneak in too? Surely you'd never miss the chance to rob a man."

His smile widened. "True, I never do. But I hear your room's small and you've seen the size of Gueulemer . . . No, I'm staying outside. I'll make sure the gentleman doesn't escape his chains . . ."

"Chains?"

"Or ropes."

"They'll bind him?"

"It's easier, that way."

"To steal?"

"To take everything." He inhaled, held the smoke in his mouth as he looked at me. "Your face . . ." He exhaled. His voice was softer. "What's happened to it?"

"Someone hit me."

"Who?"

I shrugged. "Doesn't matter. Why should it matter? What's a wounded face to you? You hurt people all the time."

"But," he murmured, "I would never hurt you."

The sleet was growing thicker now, turning to snow. It was settling on the ground. Snow seemed to make Paris look so beautiful because it covered up the dirt and it made the city look new again and I thought, *Make it better. Hide my lies. Save Valjean.*

Montparnasse came closer. "Snow . . . It must look very pretty to a girl who believes in goodness." He dropped the cigarette on to the ground, stepped on it. "It was . . . endearing," he said.

"Endearing? What was?"

"How fiery you were. When you spoke of love."

Love. We both looked out at the falling snow. I thought of Marius, holding my hand very briefly. In the Gorbeau, I could see a few candles. I said, "Will they kill this man?"

Montparnasse was quiet for a while. "They'd rather not. A body is difficult to deal with—how will they carry it, or hide it?

No, they'd prefer him to live. Perhaps they could hold him to ransom . . . He has a daughter, hasn't he?" I heard him smile—the click of lips against gums. "I can't imagine there's a single thing that a daughter wouldn't do to save her father's life . . ."

I closed my eyes. It was never meant to be like this. It was only ever meant to be a coin or two. "Montparnasse?"

"Ma belle?"

"All of this is so wrong . . ."

"Wrong? Says the girl who arranged every bit of it? *You* found this man and *you* gave him the letter. I tell you, I was impressed when I heard that, Eponine. Shall I tell you something? I was good-hearted once. Like you, I wanted to live an honest life. But then I was orphaned and Babet took care of me and he taught me all he knew . . . I owe my life to him. I think," he said, "I was born to steal. I'm made for it—as you are."

I shook my head. "I'm not made for it. I'm *not*."

"Don't pretend, Eponine. You're a Thenardier! A dishonest life is all you've ever known."

"We're Jondrettes here! That's our name!"

"You think that changes anything? *Jondrette* is just paint on rotten wood or"—he held out his hand—"snow on filthy streets. You're still a Thenardier, beneath it all . . ."

I couldn't answer him. He was right. I could never change my parentage or the name I was born with.

"As for your face . . ." He laid a single finger upon my swollen cheek. "There may be dirt and blood upon it but I know that underneath it . . . Well, you're beautiful."

I felt like crying then. I let his finger stay on me. Was he mocking me? Surely he'd seen Cosette or ladies like her, and knew what proper beauty was? Maybe he was mocking me—but it didn't really matter. Marius had made me feel beautiful but no one had called me *beautiful* in my whole life. In a tiny voice I said, "I am?"

"Oh, yes. So very beautiful . . ." He held my face with both his hands. "We'd make a fine team, Mademoiselle . . ."

"A team?"

"You and I. What couldn't be ours if we worked together? Stealing and plotting as two people, not one? I'd find diamonds for you. I'd put pearls in your ears . . ." He stroked me, almost tenderly. "I'd steal the queen's gown for my own bright queen . . ."

I closed my eyes. I had never been touched like this, like I was precious.

When I opened my eyes again, Montparnasse was looking at me in a way I recognized. It was how Marius had looked at Cosette, in Les Jardins. His eyes were bright and his lips were parted.

He took my wrist. "Come with me."

I followed him, because he'd called me *beautiful* and because I wanted Marius and because I was tired. I was so tired. He was looking at me like I'd always hoped someone would.

We went deeper into the cemetery, tripping over tree roots and broken stones. He said, "What a life we could live, you and I . . . What a world I could show you!"

Then he kissed me. But it was not a gentle kiss. Montparnasse pressed his lips against mine and clutched at my dress and he pushed me against a gravestone very roughly and his tongue filled my mouth so I couldn't breathe.

I closed my eyes and pretended this was not Montparnasse.

Pretend this is Marius, whose friends cheer when he walks into a room. But I couldn't make myself believe it. This wasn't Marius. Marius would never, ever, ever kiss someone like this.

"Get off! No!" I squirmed and broke free. I didn't want Montparnasse's mouth and hands upon me anymore, and it didn't matter that he'd called me *beautiful.* He didn't make me feel beautiful at all—just unsafe and foolish, and more alone than ever.

He didn't let me go so I kicked him.

He said, "Why, you little . . ."

Then I stamped on his foot and ran away. I leapt over the graves and stumbled through the snow and I kept running because I wanted to be free of him and my family and the name *Thenardier.*

Where was the happy life? The stars? The wayside flowers? Where was *goodness*? It was in other people, not in me. It was in Marius. In the man who'd bought Cosette a beautiful doll one Christmas Eve and said to my parents, *I'll take her to a better life.*

I'll run to the Gorbeau tenement. I'll set Valjean free. I'll shout for help— even if the Patron Minette are there. I'll fight with my father if I have to.

But I didn't get the chance because an arm caught me. It wrapped itself around my neck and pulled me to my knees and I thought, *It's Montparnasse wanting more than a kiss,* so I flailed and I bit at the arm and I shouted, "Get off!" But it wasn't Montparnasse. It was a stronger arm.

"Got you." A man's voice I didn't know.

I stopped biting and looked up. I saw a neat mustache. Two beady eyes. He was baring his teeth, and not blinking. It was a face of resentment, anger, and purpose. He wore a policeman's hat.

THE GENDARME

He lifted me from the ground by my dress so my feet pedaled the air. "You'd bite me, would you? Fight like a cat? You can't escape from me . . ."

"I thought you were . . . someone . . . else," I wheezed.

"I know who you are. You're the lookout—and a failed lookout too."

"A lookout? Monsieur, I don't know what you mean."

"Liar! I've seen you in the Gorbeau tenement with Monsieur Jondrette—if that's his proper name, which I doubt it is . . ."

"Lookout? I don't know—"

"Yes, you *do*! Do you think I'm stupid? Me, Javert? I know," he tapped his nose with his spare hand, "that you were told to stand here and keep a lookout for gendarmes like me . . ."

I couldn't keep lying. I was done with lies, so I said, "What's happened there tonight? Please tell me. Yes, I was the lookout, but I don't know anything else."

He lowered me so that my feet touched the ground but kept hold of me. "Theft. Murder. In the Gorbeau tenement."

"What? Murder? A person has died?" I wailed. "Not the man with the yellow waistcoat, Monsieur *le gendarme*? Please, not him!"

He frowned. "A yellow waistcoat? No one was wearing such a thing."

"I mean the gentleman with the kind face! The one we lured—"

"*We?* Who *we* lured?" He half smiled. "I've got my confession, it seems. No, he didn't die—although he was badly wounded. He broke from his ties and jumped from the window."

I exhaled, relieved. *Not him.* "So who? Who is dead?"

"Another."

"Which other?"

"Not a Jondrette. They've all been caught, like you. It's off to prison for your whole family now."

"Prison?"

"*Oui*—prison. I know this little trick was your idea, Mademoiselle. Your father told me so. He blames you, and your mother and sister do too."

"They blame me?"

"All your fault, they said. Said you're the worst of them." He hauled my wrists behind me and I felt handcuffs snapping on.

I gave up. I didn't fight. I was strangely calm. *It's done*, I thought. For so long we'd hidden from the gendarmerie—we'd slept in caves and moved by night and been scared of shadows. But now, it was all over. Prison had always been waiting, in the end.

The snow had never looked more beautiful than it did as we walked through it. I thought of the people I loved . . .

Gavroche, freckled and bright. Had he been lucky, after all, escaping the Thenardiers on that riverbank?

Valjean, who'd deserved so much better. *Please let him mend.* I imagined him lying by candlelight with Cosette tending to his wounds with a cloth and a basin of water.

And of course Marius. These handcuffs, his love for Cosette had changed nothing: I still loved him more than anyone else I'd ever met, even though he didn't love me, I knew that. And so I thought of him most of all as I was led away from the tenement— away from him—through the falling snow.

BOOK
FIVE

MADELONNETTES

The prison stood between the rue Volta and the rue du Vertbois, north of the river. It was made from the darkest stone I had ever seen—a sort of soot-black. It looked even darker in the snow.

Madelonnettes. It used to be a convent but I couldn't imagine nuns here. Now it was where all the worst women were taken and left, for months or years.

We went inside. A man was sitting at a table and the gendarme said, "This one's Eponine. I doubt Jondrette is her surname but write that down as well." I watched the ink write *Eponine* and I thought, *Yes, that's my name.*

They took me through the prison yard. I looked up but it was too snowy for stars. I thought of Old Auguste, at that moment. Once I'd asked him how old he was and he'd said, "Old, very old . . ."

"As old as the stars?"

"Ah, no—the stars are older than everything."

I remember thinking, *They must have seen so many sad things.* Those stars would have seen every single sin since human beings existed and yet they weren't shining above me the night I went to prison. It was as if they'd turned away from me, as if my cruelty against Valjean and Cosette had been the worst of all.

At the cell door, the policeman took off my handcuffs. A single lantern flickered on the wall. He shook his head as though all the world's problems were caused by me and said, "If you're not cured of your wickedness here, you'll never be cured."

And he pushed me into the cell, locked the door.

I was in that cell for seventeen nights. I wasn't alone. It was tiny— half the size of our room in the Gorbeau, with no hearth and no glass for the single window—and yet there were ten of us in there. I counted by the light of the candle. Nine pairs of eyes looked back at me.

It was such a small room that we sat with skin pressed against skin and I think our bodies' warmth helped us—but we still shivered. One girl's face was scarred as if by a knife; another had lice so she scratched and scratched until her skin bled. One woman rocked to herself, wild-eyed, whispering, *"Jean-Jacques? Où est Jean-Jacques?"* and then she'd search the cell for him.

We were all the same. All lost and tired.

These weren't the boasters or braggers of Paris. They weren't like my father, who'd crow about his dealings and laugh at his own tales. None of us were proud of what we'd done. Some cried, but others didn't shed a single tear in those seventeen nights that I was there. Perhaps we're born with all the tears we'll ever shed and they'd cried them all and had none left.

On a night of heavy snow, one of the women spoke to me. She was balding and had a single tooth left, peg-like. "What was it? For you?"

I sniffed, thought about my answer. "Theft. Years of it. And I had a part in a man being hurt very badly."

"Years? You're young, still."

"Sixteen, I think?" I'd lost count.

"Too young for prisons. They'll take you out. You'll see."

"Is it? My sister's in here too and she's younger still."

"Then they'll release both of you. Give it time."

"What of you?"

"Theft too. And worse. I sold what no woman should ever have to sell." I understood her meaning.

She slept—and I leaned back against the cell wall, looked out the small window at the falling snow. Was it November? I didn't know. I thought of the holly we used to have in the inn, in Montfermeil, at Christmas—when I still had warm clothes and dreams.

It snowed and snowed. Each day we'd have to push a new layer of snow off the windowsill. Our food was a half-frozen bowl of watery broth and a crust of blackened bread. We had a single shared bucket, in the corner of the cell. Sometimes we were allowed to walk out in the yard and I liked that. It was bitterly cold but it was cleaner air and I'd walk with my hands tucked under my armpits, for warmth. I looked for Maman and Azelma in the yard and I wondered if they looked for me too. Did they miss me? Or worry?

On the fifth day, I glimpsed Azelma.

I looked up and thought, *That girl looks like Azelma, but it can't be her because she's so old-looking and her hair's so thin I can see her scalp beneath it . . .* But it was her.

I stumbled. "Zel!"

She turned.

"Zel! Oh, Zel! How are you? Look at you . . . You're so thin!"

"Look at *you*," she retorted. "What a sorry state! What a mess! Look at the stains on your dress and the scabs on your face!"

I flinched, confused. Briefly I thought, *Maybe this isn't Azelma after all*, because she was being so hateful and sharp. But I saw the red wounds on her arm from where she'd punched the window-pane. She was definitely my sister. "Does it still hurt? Your arm?"

"What do *you* care?"

"You're so cross with me . . . Why?"

"Of *course* I'm cross!" she hissed. "Weren't you meant to be the lookout? Weren't you meant to be guarding your family, Eponine? Ha!" She folded her arms. "I hear you were with Montparnasse, kissing in the shadows . . . He matters more to you than *we* do, does he?"

"No, he doesn't!"

"And yet you didn't see the policemen, did you? Half a dozen gendarmes came to us, Eponine—half a dozen! They must have walked straight past you while you were having that nice little fumble in the dark . . . They came into the Gorbeau and broke the door down and arrested us." She hissed like a cat. "It was your *job* to protect us! We are all in prison because of *you!*"

I couldn't answer. My mouth opened and closed.

"You know Maman is ill?"

"Ill?"

"She's got a sickness. Nothing stays inside her—not even water."

"You've seen her?"

"A little. I've held her hand through the bars. She prefers me," said Azelma. "She always did. I'm her proper daughter."

I felt those words, like a punch. We stared at each other. Where was the thumb-sucking toddler who used to call me Ponine?

Azelma hobbled away from me. I could see her cracked heels— like hooves, as Cosette's used to be. I saw too the shape of her shoulder blades through her dress. She tried to walk with dignity— but how could she? None of us could.

That night I whispered to the woman with the peg tooth, "I've lost so much."

"You're lucky. It means you had something to lose in the first place. Me? I had nothing . . ."

That night I thought about what had been and gone. I watched the snow falling outside the cell, and remembered the swifts that darted past the inn and Azelma's doll and the outline of trees from our bedroom window. The church's smell and the butcher's dog. The owl's hoot as we ran through a nighttime field and the starriest nights I'd ever seen. The safety of the upturned boat. The hug between Cosette and her mother that rocked from side to side.

How we'd fed baby Gavroche with our milky thumbs, Cosette and me.

Life, I thought, *goes by so quickly.*

I cried a little but maybe the peg-toothed woman was right: I'd had my happy moments and my own special times. I'd known Azelma before she grew hard. I'd known how it felt to lie in the long grass with my little brother and see the blowing clouds. I thought of my mother too—twirling her skirts and saying, *Am I pretty, girls?* She hadn't always been crippled and sour, and in my head she wasn't dying of a fever in a freezing prison: She was watching her daughters swing from the rusted wagon on that bright sunny morning, after weeks of rain.

When I read her romance novels in the Sergeant of Waterloo, I sometimes found the tips of pages folded over or parts of the story underlined in ink. These were the bits she liked, I think. Beneath the rage and greed and wiry hair, maybe there was still a girl like me, who liked to dream of romance.

An End and a Beginning

She died on our final day in prison. Azelma found me in the snowy yard and said, "Maman is dead," very flatly.

I thought it wasn't true. How could it be? I could still see Maman—her puckered mouth and the dirt beneath her fingernails. How could she be gone, for always?

"Dead?"

"Yes. They've taken her body away. They'll throw her in some grave that's meant for prisoners." Still such hardness in Azelma. "Also, we're getting out."

"What?"

"They're releasing us. We're too young to be here and so tomorrow, we'll be out on the streets again."

I nodded. "What then?"

"I'll find Papa. I know which prison he's in. Babet will take care of me until Papa breaks out of there and finds me." She sniffed. "I'll live with Babet and Montparnasse. What will you do?"

I didn't know. I said, "Maybe I'll wait for Papa too," but I could tell Azelma didn't believe me. I didn't believe myself. There was a wide, wide space between myself and my family now and I thought, *He'll never forgive me for not being the lookout.* I didn't belong with them anymore. "I don't know what I'll do."

I couldn't sleep that night. The others in my cell did, coughing and moaning. But I stayed awake.

Dead. It seemed impossible. Maman had been so real and strong. How could she be lying in a pauper's grave now? But as I watched the moon come out through the cell bars, I wondered if there was a part of my mother that wasn't dead at all.

I cried for her. But then I realized I was feeling something else as well. It was strange—as if my heart and head were lighter than they'd been before.

By daybreak, I could name it. *It's relief,* I thought. I was relieved because I didn't have to steal anymore, because I didn't have to trick or lie or hand out cunning letters to the rich. I didn't have to take orders from my parents or be scared of being asked, *Well? What have you found for us? We all depend on you, you know!* I didn't have to hide my wanting heart away from them. I was free— at last.

I could actually be *me,* now. The Eponine I'd always wanted to be.

Here's what I decided, in that prison cell as the sky lightened: *I will live alone. I'll do all the good, kind acts I've ever wanted to. I won't steal. I won't lie. I'll make people's lives better whenever I can manage it. And I'll never, ever do cruel things again.*

I made another promise too. I hadn't forgotten how nasty I'd been to Cosette. As a child I had hit her and spat at her and called her names and for eight years, I'd felt the shame of it. I'd never truly gotten rid of how sorry I felt.

I'll make amends, I vowed. *Now and for the rest of my life.*

I nodded. I liked this vow.

And him? Marius. I still ached for him. But he'd called me *generous* and *smart*, and this would be enough: I'd be these things for him.

Did I still think it was unfair? That he didn't love me back? Yes, I did. I wanted him to. But I'd learned that life wasn't fair. If it was, we'd have had no need to pluck rings from fingers or buttons from coats; Widow Amandine wouldn't have been widowed; Gavroche wouldn't have been left behind. A woman called Fantine wouldn't have needed to leave her only child at an inn in Montfermeil. Cats wouldn't kill mice and leave them, uneaten. Kings wouldn't grow fat on their thrones while their people begged in their rags.

At least I'm still here, I thought then. *At least I'm still alive.*

LOOKING FOR MARIUS

The next morning we left the Madelonnettes. The ground was icy and our breath steamed.

"Well," said Azelma. "I'm off to find Papa and Babet."

"How will you live?"

She scoffed. "How we've always done, of course. Thieving never suited *you* but I'm good at it. Papa and I won't starve."

"Be careful."

"Me? Of course. I heard there are grand houses on the rue Plumet. One's got a brass knocker on its door that'll be worth a fair penny on its own. We'll go there. Plunder it."

I felt sad.

"You're not coming?" She knew I wasn't.

"No. I'm going to live on my own."

That was our good-bye—hers and mine. Azelma shrugged and turned away. She hurried down the rue Volta and was soon lost among the carriages and woodsmoke and early-morning crowds.

*   *   *

I knew what I'd do. I'd vowed to make amends to Cosette, and I wanted Marius to be happy—even though it hurt to do it. Even though my heart still whispered, *him*, and ached just to hear his name. I'd made the vow. So I had to find them.

It would be easier to find Marius. After all, I knew so many of the places he went to. The Gorbeau tenement was my starting place. I crossed the river, made my way through the streets I knew and recognized, past the church called Saint-Sulpice and the Pantheon and through the alleyways and market stalls. They were the same as ever, yet I felt different in them. I felt old, and sore inside—and I was close to tears because I loved him. But what else could I do?

I came to the tenement. Snow lay on its roof and I could see our broken window.

It felt very strange to be there again, as if a thousand years had passed, not seventeen days. I made my way up the staircase where I'd first met him and knocked on the door of Room Four.

No one answered. I glanced across to the door of Room Five and saw its wood was splintered. *From where the gendarmes kicked it down*, I thought.

Madame Bourgon was downstairs.

"Ah." Her drunken eyes. "A Jondrette. You have some nerve, girl: Your family have ruined this place. The police came, you know? To your room? There was blood and broken glass and a man called Claquesous died. A murder! In these very walls! And"—a finger came round the side of her door, pointed—"your lot owe me rent."

"Madame Bourgon, I'm so sorry for what's happened. My father's in prison and Maman has died."

"That brattish younger one?"

"Azelma won't come back here."

She puckered her mouth. "But *you're* here. Why are *you* here?" She didn't trust me any further than she'd trust a spider in a house of flies.

"To ask about the boy from Room Four. Monsieur Marius— remember? Does he still live in the Gorbeau?"

She gave a single, hard laugh. "Of course I remember. You were always mooning after him, simpering . . . Why might he or anyone still be living here, after your family's ways? They've cost me a fortune in lost rent, I can tell you. He'd been a good tenant, too—*he* always paid on time . . ."

"Do you know where he's gone?"

She scoffed. "Still following him? He wouldn't look at you twice!"

I knew this now. But still, her words were like stones thrown and I winced. "No address? Madame, is he even still in Paris?"

"Listen to me. My tenants—all of them—were so afraid that night they packed and left before sunrise, leaving nothing behind but footsteps and dust. He was the same. I don't know where he is."

With that, she slammed her door.

He wasn't there—so where? I tried to think but couldn't. My belly growled and I longed for a deep sleep.

I had no money of my own. No home to go to.

I spent the rest of the day looking for food and a sleeping place. There were alleyways but I didn't trust them and there was the wasteland but Babet prowled there sometimes. I thought of cathedrals and small churches but their doors were locked at night.

In the end, I took myself back toward the Seine. One of its bridges had a stone ledge beneath it and it looked dry. Rats scurried along the ledge but I didn't mind them. They were homeless too. Like me, they only wanted a little food and warmth.

My food was just vegetable peelings and my bed was hard and cold but, lying in it, I could see the reflections of lanterns in the water and boats passing by. *I can live a good life now.* These things were comforts to me.

I looked and looked for Marius. If he wasn't in the Gorbeau, where was he? I walked to all the places I'd ever seen him in—each street, each doorway. I went to the Jardins du Luxembourg many times in the hope he still went there. I walked the same route we'd walked that sunlit summer's evening—past the doves of Notre-Dame, and where the urchins played. In the Jardins I saw how winter turned slowly into spring because gradually, the fountain's ice melted and its tinkling sound returned. The first pale flowers pushed up.

I went to the Place de la Révolution where the guillotine stood. I didn't think he'd choose to be there—to watch lives end like that—but lots of people went there for warmth in cold weather or to buy from its stalls and so I tried it anyway. There was fish being

fried; a woman offered stockings she'd knitted—*Here, Mademoiselle!*
Cover those legs up with my stockings, see? I didn't like it there.

I went to the Café Musain too. I peered through its glass,
thinking, *Let him be inside.* There were faces I recognized—the boy
with reddish hair and the boy with half-moon spectacles on the
edge of his nose—but I couldn't see Marius. Could I go in and ask
them? I tried to—but as I pushed at the door a young man stopped
me. I'd seen him before too—the one with curly blond hair.

"Men only in Café Musain," he said.

I frowned. "But I'm looking for someone."

"All the same. Men only."

"Why?" I felt annoyed by this.

"It's how it's always been. And women don't drink ale,
Mademoiselle."

You never met Maman, I thought. "I'm looking for a boy named
Marius. Do you know him?"

"Marius?" The man looked at my clothes and my grubby hands.
Once, I might have hidden them from him but not now. There
were more important things than dirt beneath my fingernails.
"What do you want him for?"

"To speak with him—that's all. Do you know where he
might be?"

He shook his head. "I don't. I've not seen him for weeks and
I've been looking for him too. He doesn't live where he used to.
What's your name?"

"Eponine."

"If you see him, Eponine, please tell him we need him here
at the café. Tell him Enjolras and the brotherhood are making

plans and we hope he hasn't deserted us. We've got a republic to fight for."

I frowned. He didn't know me at all and yet he spoke so honestly. "How do you know I don't support the king? That I won't tell the gendarmerie about your plans?"

"Because you're so poor. No poor person could ever support this king."

Of course. Still rags and bones. Still, and always.

"You'll tell him? If you find him?"

"Yes."

"And do you have a message, Eponine? If I should see Marius before you?"

I shook my head. "No message."

An Unexpected Find

I looked for Marius but there were other people I was scared of finding. Claquesous was dead—but what of Gueulemer and Babet? I was scared of meeting Montparnasse because I'd hated that kiss against the gravestone and his hands on my bodice, and also because I'd made him so angry. What might he do, if he found me? He'd killed people, after all. So I stayed far away from the rue de la Charcuterie. If I saw a man with oiled hair or a flower in his buttonhole, I'd run.

As for Papa and Azelma, I was in two minds. Sometimes I wished Azelma could be sleeping under the bridge too. But I was also scared of meeting them. I knew they'd mock me. *Thieving never suited you*, she'd said sourly, and, *There are grand houses on the rue Plumet. One's got a brass knocker on its door . . .* Would they try to make me steal with them? I didn't want the new light in me to be put out by their darkness.

*　　*　　*

The idea came to me as I walked back from the Café Musain. I'd made vows in my prison cell—to Marius and Cosette. But hadn't I vowed to help other people too, back in the church in Montfermeil? All those years ago? I thought of the peaches. How good it felt to be kind—and I hadn't been kind for so long.

That house on the rue Plumet . . . I stopped walking. Wouldn't the kindest thing be to warn the people in it? To find the house and protect it? *Yes*, I thought, but I didn't know where the rue Plumet was. I cracked my knuckles anxiously. Paris had boulevards and alleyways and staircases and corners and rivers and parks and buildings so large that streets ran straight through them. It had whole towns within its city walls: Montmartre with its hill, the area called Montparnasse (had he been named after it? I'd never cared to ask) where the cemetery creaked with too many bones. It had more streets than I could ever count, or name. I'd never find the rue Plumet by chance.

Who could I ask? I didn't have any family now.

I tried a priest as he hurried to his prayers. "*Excusez-moi, mon Père?* Do you know the rue Plumet?" But he shook his head and moved on.

I passed a crowd of people who'd all gathered to praise Lamarque. They cheered and I pulled on a sleeve: "Monsieur? I am looking for a street named rue Plumet?" But he didn't know either.

In the end I sat down at a crossroads. From here, I could see where the Bastille prison had stood before I was born. There were lots of urchins here. They skittered between market stalls and hollered to each other and leapt over open sewers as if they had wings. I watched them for a while. Then I sighed and rubbed my eyes.

I heard, "Don't be sad, lady! At least you've still got a head on your shoulders! Many aren't so lucky . . . !" It was a child's voice—bright and bold.

I looked up.

I couldn't believe it. "Gavroche!" I cried. "Is it really you?"

Without waiting for an answer I pulled him against me and kissed into his hair and I said his name over and over. My little brother—who I'd found milk for and sung lullabies to! Who'd called me Pony and gurgled and sang!

"I thought I'd never see you again! Oh, Gavroche! Let me see you . . ." Like me, he was impossibly thin. He had scabbed knees and elbows, and his clothes were rags. His freckles were brighter against his pale skin.

He stared in disbelief. "Pony? Is it really you?"

"Yes! Yes! It's me! Oh, Gavroche . . . I've thought of you so often. You know that I never wanted to leave you on that river-bank, don't you? I tried to leap off the boat, to—"

He shrugged. "It's all right. Worse things happen."

"It *isn't* all right! It isn't at *all*! I don't know why our parents did it . . ."

"Because they didn't love me. She only wanted girls, didn't she? But that's life . . . No point being miserable!"

I couldn't believe I was looking at him. "How old are you now?"

"I'll be eight and a half next week." He seemed cheerful despite the squalor and the years that had passed between us. He glanced about. "Where are the others?"

"I'm on my own."

"They're dead?"

"Maman is. We went to prison and she died in there. She caught the disease that turns your insides to water so that it runs out of you."

"Lots of people are dying that way. It's called cholera"—he said the word very solemnly, like he was teaching me—"and it's getting worse. They reckon it'll kill you if you don't starve first! What about Papa and Azelma?"

"I don't know. Azelma said she was going to help Papa escape from prison and I didn't want to help."

"They were always close."

"They were." I smiled at him. Little Gavroche. He was eight and a half but in some ways he was like a tiny old man. "How do you live? Are you all alone?"

He grinned to show his crooked teeth. "Alone? Don't be silly! I'm not alone, Pony! Look!" And he threw his arm wide to show all the other boys who were running under carriages and sitting on walls and laughing. "See them? We're the urchins! We live together and eat together . . . It's like a family. Don't look sad! I'd rather be living with the boys on the streets than living with our parents again."

I gave a small smile. Neither he nor I were Thenardiers anymore. We were just ourselves. "You don't steal, do you?"

His smile was impish. "I try not to . . . I like to run an errand for a sou or two if I can, and there are shoes to shine and horses to brush. But I've got to steal *sometimes* . . . I try to be *nice* about it, though! I always thank them as I run away! And I don't gamble and

I don't swear. I'm quite the gentleman . . ." And he doffed an imaginary cap.

I felt so full of tenderness that I felt like crying. "Gavroche . . . there hasn't been a day that's passed where I haven't hoped you're alive and well. I'm so sorry I wasn't a better sister to you."

He swatted my words away as if they were flies that bothered him. "You weren't a bad sister. We picked blackberries together and you carried me on your back and you read stories to me—I remember that. You did what you could, didn't you? I've seen worse in this city, that's for sure, and so what's there to complain about?" He wiped his nose with his sleeve. "Anyway, I'm a rich fellow these days. There's pickings to be had at all these gatherings . . ."

"Gatherings?"

"Political." He pronounced it like *plittick-al.* "All these rallies against the king or in favor of Lamarque or whoever . . . I don't care! But people pressed together means lots of pockets to pick . . . In my gentlemanly way."

I wanted to scoop him up and keep him safe, to whisper, *Come with me; live with me. I will take care of you.* But I knew he didn't want that. He was happy as he was.

"Well, I must be off. Nice to see you, Pony." The imaginary cap was lifted again.

"Can I do anything?" I called out. "To help you? Find you food, perhaps?"

He laughed. "Food? We're roasting a whole pig over there! Stole it from the butcher's two streets away! Fancy a bit of pork in your belly?"

I laughed and shook my head. One meal for me would be one less meal for Gavroche or another urchin—and I wanted them to eat.

"Suit yourself!"

"One thing," I said, "before you go. Rue Plumet."

"Rue Plumet?"

"I'm looking for it . . ."

He didn't hesitate. "Boulevard des Invalides. Know it? Walk east along it and when you see a brick wall with ivy growing on it, turn left and that's the street you want. It goes uphill. Nice houses up there." He looked impressed. "Don't get caught . . ."

I smiled. The little brother giving out advice.

With that, he was gone. He raced among the passing cart-wheels and crowds and I felt so happy that I'd seen him. *He's alive! He doesn't hate me!* With a heart full of love for his little freckled face, I made my way toward boulevard des Invalides just as he'd told me to.

The House on the
Rue Plumet

I came to the rue Plumet at dusk.

It was a lovely part of Paris. There weren't any stalls or theaters. It was just a place full of rich people's homes and they were like no houses I'd ever seen before, with fancy curtains and decorative gates. They had dark green hedges and high gates. Inside these homes were lanterns and moving shadows—butlers or maids? Did they carry fine food on silver dishes? I could only imagine such things.

I didn't feel envious or angry anymore. My mother's order— *Always take what you can! When others are richer, make them less so*—had died with her and anyway, it hadn't ever really been what I believed.

The houses had white marble columns by their doors, like the Palais du Luxembourg. I could smell perfume and flowers. Briefly, I pretended that perfume was mine and that I was a lady with rustling skirts . . . But it felt childish now. It felt like too much had happened, and I was too old and wise to have such daydreams. Jewels and riches did not matter. Other things mattered more.

Like being kind. Like keeping people safe.

One's got a brass knocker on its door . . . Worth a fair penny on its own. That's what Azelma had said, so I eyed each door as I passed it. I found the brass knocker on the very last door of the street. It surprised me because this house was a little smaller than the others. It was half hidden from the street by an elm tree whose tiny, early buds were showing themselves, and iron railings ran all around the house.

I stepped forward.

I took hold of the railings.

This was the house they were going to plunder . . . But was I too late? Had it already been robbed? I didn't think so because a lantern burned in its doorway and the house looked peaceful: It hadn't been disturbed yet.

I must warn them. I felt nervous but I'd keep my promise. I pushed at the gate; it was locked and the railings were too high to climb. How could I get in, to tell them?

I hauled myself into the elm tree. From its higher branches I could see into their front garden and despite the late hour, it seemed full of life. Shoots were pushing up and flowers were showing themselves. A moth flittered past me and a thrush sang its evening song from the highest bough of an apple tree and I could see droplets on stalks and leaves from the afternoon's rain so that, in places, the garden shone. It was huge. And it was beautiful. A path led from the gate toward the house, past lavender bushes. The branches meant I couldn't see the front door anymore.

I sighed.

At that moment I heard a second, softer sigh. I thought it was just my echo—but there was movement. Beneath me in the garden a figure moved into view. It was a girl in a long dress and she trailed her hand over the tops of the flowers as she walked. Her pace was slow; she was in some kind of daydream of her own.

Still sighing, she walked through the garden's shadiest part away from me. I waited in my elm tree—and before long she came back, walking toward me, still in the shade, holding a single bloom of honeysuckle—smelling it and turning it between her thumb and forefinger.

I wonder if I knew already. I've heard people talk of intuition, an inner voice that whispers the truth to you before you're shown it. Some people think it's the voice of God—but what about the people who say there isn't a God at all? And what of animals? Because I've seen birds take cover in the moments before a hawk flies by, and the old gray nag seemed to know when I carried an apple in my pocket. There's a knowing with the heart, I think— just as much as there's a knowing with the head.

My heart knew. Even before she stepped into the lantern's light I knew this girl was Cosette.

I also knew who she was thinking of. I knew why she sighed and why she was holding the honeysuckle like it was made of silver or gold.

She was in love with Marius, just like I was. The only difference was that he loved her back.

The Girl in the Garden

Her dress was taffeta and it trailed on the ground. Her hair was unpinned. It was longer than it ever was in Montfermeil, reaching down to her waist.

Cosette lives here. In a house that matched her beauty. And Valjean . . . ? Was he still alive? He must have been wounded very badly at the Gorbeau; what if he'd died afterward? I leaned forward and peered through the branches of the elm tree, seeking a man's silhouette. I scanned the windows of the house—all dark except one where a candle was shining.

I thought of the Louis d'or, placed in her shoe. His face as he'd read the letter in Les Jardins du Luxembourg and the concern on it.

It will be my fault if he's dead.

I closed my eyes. I could hear the soft pad . . . pad . . . of Cosette's feet as she walked. With all my heart I hoped that Valjean was still alive and I whispered to myself, "Let him be, let him be . . ."

Then I saw him.

I nearly called out in relief! It was Jean Valjean, standing by the window with the candle. I knew his silhouette, his hair and shape. But he seemed to be standing awkwardly, as if leaning on a stick, like Maman used to do. With his spare hand, he rapped on the glass.

Cosette looked up.

"I'm coming, Papa!" she called, and she hurried back through the garden past the apple tree, dropping the honeysuckle as she went.

Their house. It was where the two people I'd hurt the most in my life lived. If I wanted to make up for my past mistakes, my past choices, this was the time.

I will not let them be robbed. I'd do whatever it took it protect them because I was the new, free, kind Eponine who wasn't being told to steal anymore. And I knew that Marius's heart would break if she, Cosette, was hurt at all. I would protect them.

So I no longer slept beneath the bridge with the reflections and the rats. I chose the elm tree, instead. There was a fork in its branches that I'd wedge myself into so that I couldn't fall out, and I slept among its new, growing leaves. This way, I could guard them. If Azelma and Papa were going to burgle this house they'd do it at night. They'd creep up the dark side of the street with a finger pressed to their lips—Shh . . .—and I could drop down from the branches and say, *Stop!*

In my new leafy bedroom, there were moth wings and insects and sometimes a bird would perch, clean its wings. How could this be Paris? Where sewage ran down streets and people fought and the disease called cholera was leaving bodies in the gutters or lying outside hospitals. It was peaceful up here, like a different world.

My elm-tree nights. I half slept, half listened for my sister's light tread on the ground. But by day I still looked for Marius. I just wanted to see his face again and so I returned, over and over, to the Café Musain. I trailed my fingers along the railings of the Jardins du Luxembourg, looking through them. I peered down every alleyway and went to rallies in the hope that he might be the man chanting, *"Vive Lamarque! Bring in a republic!"* I hoped for his soapy scent or a glimpse of his woolen coat but I only found strangers jostling and cursing and standing on chairs. I covered my nose because I didn't want to catch the disease that killed Maman and lots of others.

Sometimes in my elm tree, I thought he might come here. Because if he knew that Cosette lived on the rue Plumet, surely he'd come every day? But he never did. *Which means,* I soon realized, *that he doesn't know. He's got no idea that she lives here at all. But I could tell him. When I find him . . .* And I liked this idea because it would make him happy. I could make him smile.

Spring bloomed on. The garden beneath me unfurled its petals and leaves, and as I was looking down at it—at all its flowers like tiny faces—I spotted a strange flower. It was dark red, almost purple. It was like a rose but not a rose. Where had I seen it before?

In a cottage garden. In Austerlitz. The garden of an old man called Mabeuf. He'd had white bristles and a hunched back. I'd forgotten all about him!

He'll know where Marius is.

I ran there. It was a warm afternoon. I remembered the way—running past the tanneries and on to an earthy lane. I only paused to drink from a fountain and wash my face in it.

The cottage was the same and its garden was still overgrown, full of beetles and vines and bright flowers. Mabeuf was there. He was dozing on a bench in the late-afternoon sun. His mouth was open and I could hear him snoring.

Part of me wanted to shake him awake and say, *Where is Marius?* But he was old and looked very peaceful. I wanted to let him sleep.

I trod down the garden path, through the greenery. The sun was dipping slowly. Soon, the first chill of evening would creep into the garden and the flowers would creak shut. A watering can sat by the house, filled up. Perhaps he had been too tired to tend to his garden, too sore in his bones?

I make people's lives better these days. So as Monsieur Mabeuf slept, I watered every plant he had. Who knew what was happening elsewhere in the world, at that moment? Fires and sickness and loss? In the middle of Paris, people would be shaking their fists at the word *king* and saying, *"Fight, fight!"* But I was just watering an old man's garden, tending to his daisies and his strawberry plants. I hummed happily. There's such a peace in small, kind things. I imagined the earth drinking and saying, *Thank you, Eponine.*

After a while, he woke. He yawned and stretched, and through half-closed eyes he spied me.

"What . . . ? Who are you?"

"Monsieur," I said. "Excuse me for intruding but I'm looking for Marius? I know you're friends so maybe you can help me?"

"Marius?"

"The young gentleman? It's very important."

The man shifted. "Yes. He comes here often. But mostly Marius spends his days in a field near Les Invalides—a meadow. He goes there to think, for he has plenty on his mind." Mabeuf blinked around him. "My flowers. You watered them?"

With that, I was gone. I thanked him and hurried away so that all I left behind me was damp soil and sucking plants. I wondered later if Mabeuf might think he had imagined me—a little thing in rags who'd hummed and watered his garden before slipping away (*she was like a sprite, or a ghost of some kind!*) into the gathering dusk.

THE BLOWING FIELD

Night fell before I could find this field. I returned to the elm tree and nestled in, thinking, *Tomorrow I'll see him.* It'd been nearly half a year since I last had. Autumn leaves had been blowing. He'd been looking over the top of his book at a girl who wasn't me.

Marius.

I felt afraid as I sat in the darkness. I longed to see him but I also knew that the past few months had changed me. What if they'd changed him too? Or what if he'd learned that the trouble in Gorbeau that night had all been my idea? He'd hate me. He'd turn his back on me.

I didn't sleep at all. When the sky started to lighten I made my way toward the field that Mabeuf had told me about. It wasn't very far from the rue Plumet. I looked across the rooftops of Paris as I went. The distant hill of Montmartre was lit by morning sun.

I'd seen far nicer meadows. During my running days, I'd seen fields filled with poppies and anemones and woodbine, with butterflies flitting through them. *But*, I thought, *this is Paris*. It was a dirty, crowded city with no butterflies in it at all.

I was still a long way away when I realized he was there, that it was definitely him. He was sitting down against the wooden fence like a farmer's son, his hands in his pockets. For a moment he wasn't the well-dressed gentleman with a book in his hand but just a boy with messy hair and his shirtsleeves rolled up.

I approached him slowly. Everything inside me was fluttering like wings.

"Monsieur Marius?"

He stood and turned, surprised. He took his hands from his pockets and stepped back from me. A shadow passed behind his eyes and I thought, *He knows. He knows that night was my idea.*

"You," he said. He looked disappointed and mistrustful too. It made me tearful to see it; I didn't want him to look at me this way.

I held out my hands, as if to reassure him. "Oh, Marius! Please don't think badly of me or judge me. It wasn't all my fault, I swear it!"

"Isn't that all we have? To judge a person by their actions?"

"Perhaps. But a person can make mistakes and people can change too."

"Our walk back from Café Musain that evening . . . You seemed so . . . gentle. We talked of dreams . . . It was a lovely walk, wasn't it?"

"Yes."

"And then I learn that you lured a man to the tenement! I heard him calling for help, Eponine! He was in fear for his life so I ran into the corridor and was about to break down your door when the police came." He shook his head. "They meant to *kill* him. And it was all your idea? I heard your family saying so, as they were taken away. Have I completely misunderstood who you are?"

"No, you haven't! Not at all! And it was never my idea to hurt a single soul! Maybe I thought we could get money from him, I admit that—but I never meant for him to go to the Gorbeau or be so hurt or so afraid. Marius, I'll regret my part in that terrible night for the rest of my life. That's the truth."

He thought about this. "You went to prison, I hear?"

I nodded. "We all went. Maman died inside. Azelma and I were released because we were too young to be there."

He seemed to soften then. His frown went away. He gave a single nod, as if understanding me, and sighed heavily. "Your father's the true villain in your family, I think."

"He's meant to be in prison for years and years—but Azelma said she'd help him escape."

"And has she?"

"I don't know. I've not seen them since and don't want to. I don't want to live that life anymore, Marius. Can you believe me? All I've ever wanted is something better."

He tilted his head, like he often did. "Yes, Eponine . . . I can believe you. Poverty makes people act against their heart, I know. People must make hard choices, just to survive." He took a step toward me and touched my arm as if consoling me. I filled up with relief—*He doesn't hate me.* "Where are you living, now?"

"A tree."

"What?"

I smiled. "I know. But it's clean and safe, and I haven't fallen out yet."

Did he smile too? I couldn't tell because he looked away. "You're right, Eponine. A person can change very suddenly. They can change in a moment . . ."

"You've changed too?"

"Yes. Not through prison, I've never been to prison. But I've changed through something else—which is perhaps like a prison in how tightly it keeps hold of me. Sometimes I can hardly breathe! I can't do a single thing without thinking of her."

I stood very still.

"I'm captured by her. By love . . ."

I whispered, "I know."

"You know? About love?"

His surprise stung me. "I know I wear rags and I'm skinny and knotty-haired, and I know I've done bad things in my life—but this doesn't mean that I don't know what love is."

"Really? You've been in love?"

"Is it so hard to imagine? Just because I am thin and poor . . ." I paused, a little breathless. I was scared to say the words, but I managed them. "I love someone so much it hurts."

"I know that love! That's the love I feel!"

I gave him a smile but I knew it was a sad one. It was all I could manage.

"I'm sorry," he said. "For thinking so badly of you. I heard your parents blaming you and so I assumed . . . But I believe you now, Eponine. I know you had no wish to hurt Valjean that night. You wouldn't do such a thing."

Now I nearly laughed with relief. But I had to add one more thing: "When we walked back through Paris, from the Café Musain, I wasn't pretending to be someone else. That was me."

He smiled. "I know. I liked her."

We stood as the sun rose higher. If I'd stretched out, I might have touched him, but I didn't. I took a deep breath. I knew it would hurt but I had to ask: "So . . . who is she? This girl you love so much?"

"I don't know her name," he said, his face lighting up. "But I saw her for the first time in the summer—the day after our evening walk! The next day! I'd walked to the Jardins du Luxembourg— do you know them?—to read, and I looked up from my book . . . At first, I didn't think she was truly beautiful: She didn't capture my heart as soon as I saw her. But I couldn't stop watching her, all the same—as if there was something of greater beauty to her than her face alone. Her soul? Her spirit? Then she looked up and saw me—and I wondered if I was looking at a part of me I hadn't known I'd lost but had found now, because I felt like I *knew* her! When she looked at me, she became beautiful. Our eyes met and my heart filled up . . . Oh, it was exactly like you said! I felt so full of love I could barely hold it in! From then on, she has been all I can think of . . . The months have passed but my love hasn't faded. I think of her as I walk or eat or read . . . I have thought of her when I was with my friends at the Café Musain . . . even as the crowds have been shouting about revolution and Lamarque and changing France all I can think of is her, her, her. I used to take myself off to Les Jardins so many times, hoping she'd be there—and often she was. But she was always with a man—her father, I think . . . Then I saw her father in the Gorbeau tenement on that awful night—the night you were part of!—and I've not seen her since. Has she left Paris? I'm so scared she has! I walk the streets looking for her, Eponine! I search markets and churches, and I look for her bright hair! And I come to this field because I overheard her speaking about it, once—a meadow near Les Invalides with cornflowers in it . . . This must be the place, mustn't it? Look at the flowers!" He paused, rubbed his eyes with his knuckles.

He'd never said so much to me.

I felt so much pain inside me that I thought I might cry. It was a proper pain, like someone had taken a knife and stabbed me. I thought I might fall down in that field. Instead, I closed my eyes and I thought, *Make him happy.*

I had to try. "Marius?"

"Hm?" He sounded so tired.

With shaking words, I whispered: "I know her name. It's Cosette."

He looked up. "What? You know her?"

I nodded.

"How? How on earth can you know who I love?"

"I saw you. In the Jardins du Luxembourg. I know the lady you were looking at."

He blinked. "You do? You know her? But she is so elegant and well dressed! She's a lady! How . . . ?"

I knew how it seemed. Her and me. Like sun and rain. "She was named Euphrasie at birth but no soul has ever called her that. She's always been Cosette."

His eyes flashed and he took my wrists. "My God! How . . . ? Speak to me!"

He clutched my wrists to his chest as if they were all that mattered to him, my wrists and nothing else. His eyes were bright and his breath was warm upon my face.

"We grew up together," I said, trying to stop myself trembling. "It's hard to believe, I know, for she is so beautiful and I'm not, but we were raised in the same house. In a village called Montfermeil."

"Montfermeil . . . ," he repeated dreamily. "How? How did it happen?"

"Her mother was very poor. She was destitute. Abandoned by her husband, I think, and she couldn't work and care for the child. So she left Cosette with my parents. She paid my parents to clothe her and feed her and house her . . ." I looked down. I couldn't tell him anymore.

"And the man who's always with her? You say she has no father . . ."

"He came one Christmas. He said that Cosette's mother had died, and her dying wish had been for him to care for her only child. So he came to Montfermeil and paid a fine sum to my parents for her. He bought her a doll."

"Paid your parents? Why did he pay them?"

I winced. "She'd worked for them. She'd been very useful and they wanted . . . compensation . . ."

Marius understood me. He shifted his jaw. "When was this?"

"We were nine, or nearly. So long ago."

He let go of my wrists, exhaled. "And he has cared for her ever since?"

"I think so."

"And has she been happy?"

"I can't imagine she's wanted for anything."

"And tell me: is she"—he paused, swallowed as if the words were hard for him—"betrothed at all?"

"I can't be sure of my answer. But no, I don't think she is."

I hesitated, then. I knew there was more to say, that she loved him too—but I felt scared of saying it. I felt scared because then he'd leave me; he'd run from this field and my life, looking for her, and what if he never saw me again? Never even remembered me? Lived his whole life with only Cosette on his mind, for always? These felt like my last few moments with him.

Marius. My love for him would never stop. He had my heart and always would—but his heart, I knew, was not mine.

I took a deep breath. "She thinks of you, Marius—just as you think of her . . ."

Marius gasped. He seized my wrists again. "What? What? Oh, how do you know this? Does she speak to you?"

"No, but I've seen her. I can tell . . ."

"Oh!" He smiled a wide, bright smile and looked up at the sky as if thanking it. He held my wrists so tightly that I could feel my heartbeat thumping there, beneath his hands. "Where is she, Eponine?"

"On the rue Plumet."

He let go of me. I stumbled back from his grasp, and knew that his world was different now. I'd changed it with my words and it had been so hard to do. He pushed his hands up into his hair and he did this in the way I'd always wanted to do with my own hands, into the very roots of his hair. "Cosette! What a name . . ."

I had come this far. I had to tell him everything, so I said, "The house isn't far. Shall I take you there?"

"Would you do that? For me?"

I thought, *Of course.* I'd do anything in the whole world for him, however much it hurt.

One Last Walk

We walked side by side. He wanted to walk very quickly but I didn't because I wasn't sure when I'd get the chance to walk with him again. I listened to his footsteps and his breathing. He swung his hands as he walked and I thought of Monsieur and Madame Lefevre, back in Montfermeil, always holding hands.

"I've been looking for you a long time," I whispered. "Six months."

"What?" He looked shocked. "Six months?"

"Maybe five. A long time, anyway."

"Why?"

"In prison, I made a promise to myself—to be kind, where I could. I thought you would be happier if you knew where Cosette lived. So I had to find you."

He smiled in disbelief. "But you hardly know me. And how did you find me? Where did you look?"

"I asked people. I went to the Gorbeau. I'd seen you in the Jardins du Luxembourg so I went there too. The Café Musain, of course."

"The Musain? You went there? It's men only."

"I know. A friend of yours wouldn't let me inside. His name was Enjolras and he told me to tell you me that they're making plans and need you back." I glanced across. "What plans?"

He pressed his lips together for a moment. "Enjolras wants a fairer France as we all do. The rich are so wealthy that their ceilings are gold-painted and yet the poor are so poor they're eating dirt in the street—how's that fair? How can we have a king with diamonds and rubies and his huge, powdered wig, when people don't have bread?" He shook his head. "Our country needs changing. Lamarque will change it. We'll fight the king's armies in the street until they're defeated and Lamarque can take over, and make France a republic again."

I felt uneasy. "You'll fight? In the street? But the armies have cannons and muskets . . ."

"We've got muskets too. And we will build barricades to protect us."

"But what if you're wounded? You might die!"

"Some will die, I'm sure of it. There are always deaths, in a war. But, Eponine, shall I tell you the truth? Last summer, I'd have fought a thousand wars for France. I told you, didn't I? That I was patriotic?"

"And now?"

He sighed. "Now . . . well, I still love France. The revolution *must* happen, Eponine, I still believe in that! But now that I know what love is . . . How could I risk my life? Now that I know Cosette exists?"

I looked away. *He won't fight or die.* That was a comfort, at least.

We walked in silence the rest of the way. But in my head there were so many words turning over and over that I couldn't be sure which words to take out and whisper to him. I wanted to tell him how often I'd followed him. How Paris seemed so much better once I knew he was in it. I wanted to tell him about the Lefevres, as alike as their chimneys. And I wanted to say, *Someone tried to kiss me and I pretended it was you but I just felt sad. I wished it was you.*

But I didn't say these things. Of course not.

"Here we are."

"This is it? Where she lives?" He walked toward the gate and shook it. "It's locked—locked! How can I get to her?"

"We wait."

"Wait?"

"She walks in the garden every evening."

"What time?"

"Early. As the birds are roosting."

"How long must we wait, then? Five hours? Six?"

His impatience hurt me and I felt my lip tremble. *How I wish it was me he wanted to see.* But I managed to smile. "Maybe. But we can sit in this elm tree and rest . . ."

He paused, looked up. "That's the tree you sleep in?"

"Yes. My little home."

He half smiled. "It's a good tree. But I'll stand beneath it, I think, because I don't want to tear my clothes on it or make them dirty . . ."

He wanted to look smart for her. I ached—but I understood.

I climbed into the branches and looked down on his thick, soft hair. And we waited for her, Marius and I. The hours passed, and I knew those hours were my only chance to share my heart with him. If I was ever going to tell Marius that I loved him and that he'd changed my whole world, then it was now, as I sat in the tree. *But he loves Cosette.* What good would it do? I kept my heart to myself.

I liked being high in the branches. I felt safe, as if the tree was cradling me and saying, *Don't be sad, Eponine. Poor thing* . . . But also, I felt like I could protect him. No harm could come to him— no guns or soldiers or cholera—if I was looking down on him like the stars look down on all of us.

After awhile, those stars came out.

Marius glanced up. "It's getting dark. The birds are roosting, Eponine. Will she come now?"

We both heard the sound. It was the *shush* . . . *shush* . . . of skirts and it came nearer.

He moved forward and took hold of the iron gates again. I saw her through the branches and she looked more beautiful than ever. Her dress was powder-blue and her hair had ribbons in it and she carried a fan, its fine strap looped over one wrist.

"Cosette!" he called out.

She jumped. She dropped the fan and didn't pick it up again. Instead, she pressed her hands to her mouth and stared at him. "Can it be . . . ?"

"It *is* your name? Cosette?"

"It is! And what's yours?

"Marius."

She came closer. "Marius . . ."

"For so long, you're all I've thought about."

"And all I've thought about," she whispered, "is you."

Long, long ago I was walking near the church in Montfermeil. It must have been midsummer because the air was thick with heat and the sun was so bright I was squinting and as I paused, a butterfly—white with orange tips—settled on my arm. I was so amazed by this little thing of beauty that I could hardly breathe because what if my breathing disturbed it, and it flew away? I didn't even blink because it was so beautiful.

They were like that.

Cosette unlocked the gate and let him in. In the garden, they looked at each other and gently took each other's hands.

I stayed in the shadows. This was their moment, not mine. As I watched them, a tear rolled down my cheek, and then another.

Without taking their eyes off each other, they walked toward the house and stepped inside.

Yes, a person can change. It can happen with the smallest of things—and I might have had a good heart, but I still felt so sad that I thought my body would break with it. He was gone. He was hers. All those dreams I'd had—what good were they now?

But you've brought him happiness, Eponine; he is happy because of you—and that was my only comfort as I cried and cried, feeling so lonely, in my house of leaves.

The Days and the Nights

He left at sunrise. He crept beneath my tree without looking up. From one of the windows Cosette watched him go.

I slid down the trunk and spent the rest of the day in the city because, for the first time in so long, I could walk its streets without having to look for him. I didn't have to search crowds for his voice or his dimpled smile. I could simply walk where I chose to. So I went to Montmartre, Les Champ de Mars, and Bastille. I went to the place de la Révolution where the guillotine used to be. For decades, its blade had dropped onto neck after neck in that square but it had been moved now, and so the place de la Révolution was empty. A few crows called out. I stood and thought, *So many people died here . . .* These rooftops would have been the last thing they ever saw, before kneeling.

Late May. Paris was hot and crowded. Anger spilled out of bars into alleyways, and the fever that killed Maman was everywhere. The girl I'd been in Montfermeil, who'd longed for a dainty, romantic Paris . . . Where had she gone? She was all grown up. She was wearing rags and stepping over bodies. *Wise Eponine . . .*

That evening I went back to the tree—I couldn't help it—and watched them walk in the garden. She said, "I was scared you'd gone, and wouldn't come back."

"I'll always come back," he said.

I cried very quietly, into cupped hands.

He did come back—night after night. And I always kept guard, because for all the talk of love and night-scented flowers I'd not forgotten my vow or Azelma's words: *We'll plunder it.*

I wouldn't let it happen. I was ready for them.

BEAUTIFUL EPONINE

They came on a moonless night. I parted the leaves and saw the dark sky, and I felt uneasy. Papa always said, *Pick a moonless night . . . Don't let yourself be seen!*

I told myself, *There are many dark nights. It might not be tonight.*

But it was.

I heard footsteps in the street below. They were soft and slow, the kind we make when we don't want anyone to hear us. I shifted and saw them: shadows against the wall. Was there a flash of metal?

I dropped down from the tree. It made them jump because they'd thought they were all alone but there I was. I landed like a cat—neatly, claws out.

"What the . . . ?" It was Papa's voice. "Is that *Eponine*?"

"Papa." I was cool.

"Well . . . !" He relaxed, half laughed. "Why are *you* here?"

Another voice came from the shadows. It was Montparnasse. "Well, well. Perhaps she has come to help us, Luc?" Behind him I could make out the shadow of Gueulemer—darker, even, than the night.

There was no warm greeting from Papa. The last time I'd seen him had been all those months ago in the Gorbeau tenement, as he sent me outside to keep watch by the cemetery. Since then I'd been in prison, and Maman had died. Had he looked for me at all? Wondered how I was?

He said, "Do you know this house? We've heard it's worth robbing."

I could smell Babet beside me—tobacco and ale and unwashed clothes. "Silver candlesticks, we hear," he murmured. "Hand mirrors, furs, silk underclothes . . ."

"Why this house? There are bigger ones."

"They had a maid here for a while. Montparnasse knew her, didn't you?" Babet snickered. "She told him all about it—where they keep their jewels and money . . ."

Papa spat, wiped his mouth. "You'll help us, Eponine. Not as lookout, though—you've proved to be useless at that . . . Azelma is our lookout tonight."

"Azelma's here?"

"At the top of the road."

I looked at Montparnasse. He wasn't smiling. His hair wasn't oiled and he wasn't wearing a flower in his buttonhole. He was staring at me very darkly. I'd run away from him, and I wondered how many girls had ever managed to do that before? Not the maid, anyway.

Four of them. They carried sticks and rocks and blades.

"No."

Papa flinched. "What?"

"No, I won't help you."

He blinked, licked his lips, and gave a soft chuckle. "She's always had humor, my eldest daughter—I'll give her that!" Then his laughter faded. "You *will* help us, Eponine."

"No, I won't. I won't do a single thing to help you—not tonight, not ever."

He wanted to hit me, I could tell. He hissed and his eyes flamed, and he said, "How dare you? You're my *daughter*! It is your *duty*!"

I felt fiery too. "Your daughter? Yes—by birth alone! You made me, that's true, but have you ever been fatherly in any other way? Loving or caring? Have you ever hugged me or told me a bedtime story or looked after me when I was sick or scared? Ha! You've only ever liked me when I've had a fistful of coins or a pocket watch for you. You never wanted a daughter: You wanted a helper, a thief, a servant you can give orders to. Well, not anymore! I've been in prison, Papa! It's been many months since you saw me but you've not asked how I am or how I'm living or if I'm missing Maman! And as for Gavroche—how *could* you? What parent leaves a child behind—a tiny child!—and doesn't care? I'd like to think you had a little kindness in you, Papa, but I've never seen it and I know I never will."

He was furious but I kept talking.

"You think I'm still the little girl who used to creep between the legs of drinkers, in the inn? I've grown up! I'm old enough to know my own heart and mind, and I will never, *ever* steal or lie again. Do you know how I feel when I see you? All of you? I feel *ashamed*. And I feel *disgusted*—I'm disgusted in how you never care for others, and all you ever do is steal . . . In Montfermeil we could have lived an honest life! But you gambled and robbed . . ." I shook my head. "Do you know how I felt when I'd heard that Maman had died? Sad—but I felt relieved too—*relief!*—because I could start again. Live the kind of life I've always wanted. Sometimes Maman could be loving. But you, Papa? I don't think you have any idea what love feels like—and that makes me pity you."

All four of them were staring at me.

"I've two more things to say to you. First, I'm not going to let you rob this house. It won't happen."

It was Montparnasse who spoke. "There are four of us and one of you. You think you can stop us?"

"Yes, Monsieur. Because you might have knives and stones but I have a voice and if you take one step closer to me, or to these iron gates, I'll scream so loudly that every soul on the rue Plumet will wake up and the gendarmes will find you. I promise."

"And second?" muttered Papa. His eyes were hateful.

"This is the last time I will ever call you my father. After tonight, you're just a stranger to me."

I was defiant. I was the strong, bold heroine of all Maman's books, the girl with blowing hair and her hands on her hips, and I felt so bright and strong. No, they wouldn't pass. Evil wouldn't win. I'd scream till daybreak, if I had to.

"Bitch," Papa said, very quietly. That was his last word to me.

*   *   *

Then they turned and left. They padded up the rue Plumet into the darkness, and I was left alone. *I have no family now.* It was just me and the night air, but the world seemed to be whispering, *Well done, well done, well done!*

I stayed awake in my tree, and watched the sky lighten.

At daybreak, I walked back toward the river. I passed tavern owners and old wives sweeping, and a man picking out the hooves of his horse—and I bid all of them, *"Bonjour. C'est un joli matin, non?"* They seemed surprised, but said, *"Bonjour,"* back to me. A baker offered me a bread roll and my *merci* was grateful and bright.

On a bridge, I looked down into the river. The reflected girl had dirt on her face as always, but she was smiling. She was eating a bread roll and her hair was blowing about her and I thought, *Maybe she's beautiful?* Yes, I thought she was.

I walked through a sun-dappled Paris.

Oui. Un très joli matin.

BOOK
SIX

AZELMA

When I was a little girl I used to think that when it rained, it was the sky crying. If I was crying at the same time, I wondered if the rain was coming down in sympathy, matching my feelings, saying, *There, there . . .*

It was like that in Paris, that day. But it wasn't raining: Instead, it was the hottest day I'd ever known. I sweated under my arms and my skin turned red. *The world is burning*, I thought. *Like I burned inside, last night.*

It meant the streets smelled more than ever. They stank of sweat and sewage and rotting meat. Dogs panted for water. Tempers were like tinder so that the tiniest thing sparked them and people brawled in the street. Near the Tuileries one man stabbed another; I heard the scream and I saw his blood flowing out.

"This is dangerous weather," somebody said.

The cholera was even worse. It had always been there in the shadows but now people were squatting in the gutters or vomiting in corners. Bodies were left outside the morgue. I held my breath as I passed them and thought of Gavroche because some of the bodies were child-sized.

Please let him be safe—and please let Marius and Cosette and Jean Valjean be safe. And the man who gave me chestnuts.

And Azelma. I thought of her too. So she had been standing on guard last night, at the end of the rue Plumet? Their new, better lookout. She'd gotten as hard as stone but she was still my sister and so I thought, *Keep her safe too.*

I sent small prayers out for everyone I cared for, and for the people that *they* cared for too. But I forgot about the man called Larmarque. I forgot to whisper, *Keep him safe from this fever.* Could I have saved him? If I had whispered it?

On June 1 he died. And if the city had been hot and angry before, it really caught fire with this.

I heard the news in Les Halles. Just as fires snicker from twig to twig and get stronger and louder, so this news moved through the crowd . . . *Lamarque! Dead! The cholera's got him! What now? What now?*

I thought of Marius and his curly-haired friend in Café Musain who had called Lamarque *the man who will save us.* The market swarmed and wailed.

Within days, the gunshots began. I was near the Café Musain when I heard them and dropped to my knees. "What's that?" I cried out.

A man helped me up. "Soldiers."

"Why are they shooting?"

"There are riots already. You know Lamarque's dead? There's no one to fight for the people now and so the people are having to fight themselves. I'd leave here," he said. "It'll only get worse."

I thanked him and hurried on. Marius and Cosette were safe, weren't they? Holding hands in the rue Plumet and not here, on the streets? But I was scared. I ran down the rue de la Chanvrerie and straight into a girl.

She shouted, "Hey! Watch it!" It was Azelma.

We stared.

I hadn't seen her since we left prison and she looked much older now. There were lines by her eyes, and bruises. Her hands were tightly closed so I knew she'd been stealing—centimes, perhaps. There couldn't be much left to steal anymore.

"Azelma! How are you? Are you well? No fever?"

"Do I *look* as if I've got the fever?" Still sour.

Perhaps the question was stupid but I didn't blush. "Where are you living?"

She didn't answer. Instead she said, "Papa told me what you said to him, the other night. We *disgust* you, do we?"

"Not you, Zel. Papa. The others. Do you think he's ever really loved us?"

She hardened her jaw, defiant. "Perhaps he never loved *you*. But he loves *me*."

"Does he act like he does?"

She looked a little sad for a moment. "What does love matter anyway? It doesn't feed or clothe you. That house? In the rue Plumet? The things inside it could have fed us for a month!"

"But the people who live there are good people! They've had their own suffering and don't deserve more."

"Their own suffering? They're rich! And we're not! What do *I* care about their suffering? I could be wearing silk dresses now . . ."

"So you're happy to steal all your life?"

"It's a cruel world and we must be cruel to survive it." I heard our mother's voice in that.

"Look at me, Azelma: I'm surviving it! But I haven't stolen anything since I left Madelonnettes. I beg or I scavenge but I don't steal, and I haven't done a single cruel thing—and I'm *happier* for it! Oh, Zel . . ."

Suddenly, she softened. She looked her age, which wasn't old at all. "Do you think we're the only ones living like this? Didn't you hear the gunshots? Worse things are happening in Paris than a stolen sou or two. Stealing's what I know. It's what I'm good at and it's what Papa and Montparnasse want me to do."

"Montparnasse?" I frowned. Why would she do what he wanted of her? Then I guessed: *She likes him.* Perhaps she hadn't run away from his mouth, as I'd done. Perhaps she actually wanted to feel those hands . . .

I loved my little sister then. I wanted to whisk her up in my arms and take her far away from there—from diseases and prisons and the city's heat. "Do you remember your doll?" I asked.

"My doll?"

"We used to play with her . . . remember?" I reached for Azelma's hair and stroked it. "Shall we go somewhere? You and me? We could leave Paris and head south, follow the sun . . . Maybe we can find a little work picking fruit or pressing grapes

236

into wine with our feet, or plucking hens . . . An honest life. A better life than this."

She moved my hand away. "And what of Papa? I won't leave him. You might think he's a disgrace but I don't. I'll stay with him, and with Montparnasse, and if you really hope for a good, honest life then I'm telling you, Eponine, you will *fail*. Haven't you seen? There are riots! A revolution is coming, and no one will care for your high morals! What matters is blood and anger, kings and the rest of us. Everyone hates one another and it'll be a fine time for stealing—all these gatherings. You'll miss out," she said, and stepped back.

We looked at each other. I remembered how we used to sleep together in Montfermeil, under the same blanket. Her little pops of sleeping breath. Her warm body pressed against my own. I felt sad.

"Be careful." In my head I thought, *Find love. Fall in love with someone who's worth it—for it changes everything.*

She sniffed. "I'm going to where the gunshots came from. Newly dead men are easy to rob."

Oh, she was our father's daughter.

"You know that you've angered them? By defending that house? They *will* steal from it, Eponine—and they'll hurt everyone inside it too. You can't defend it forever."

With that, she went. She moved through the crowds until she was lost among them, and I wanted to call out, *I love you!*—because I did. But she moved too quickly.

I had a strange feeling, at that moment. I felt, in my bones, that my sister was gone now and that I'd never see her again.

* * *

Azelma was wrong in a lot of what she said. But one thing stayed with me: *You can't defend it forever.*

I sat in the elm tree that night. Somewhere beneath me, Paris glowed with fires and the flashes of gunshots. Tomorrow they'd bury Lamarque. I couldn't imagine a quiet funeral procession—nobody could. There'd be trouble, I was sure of it.

I wanted to warn Cosette and Valjean, to knock on their door and say, *Do you remember the people who hurt you, Monsieur? In the Gorbeau? Well, they're coming back to take everything you have and to hurt you again . . .* But those tall iron gates were always locked. I wanted Cosette to walk back out through the dusk so that I might shout out to her—but she was always inside, these evenings. She was no longer lovesick, sighing in the dark; she had Marius now.

I rubbed my eyes, tearful. Why did things always have to be so hard?

But then among the gunshots and dogs barking and distant calls for help, I heard another sound. It was the skittering of paper. Beneath me, a tiny piece of newspaper blew by.

I'll write a note! I grabbed the paper and walked until I found a little bit of charcoal and then I wrote: *"You're in danger. The villains from the Gorbeau know you live here and are coming again. Be careful."*

I dropped it through the iron railings, into the garden. It lay next to the lavender bush so I knew it would be found—my little act of love.

Two Good Hearts

The following morning I woke and looked down through the elm tree to see if the note was still lying there beside the lavender. It wasn't. It had been found and read.

I was glad. I climbed down and stretched. But I stopped, mid-stretch—because the house looked different. There weren't any drapes at the windows anymore and there were suitcases and boxes on the path, outside. Then I turned to see a carriage waiting in the street with a gray horse dozing by it.

I hurried to the driver. "*Excusez-moi?* Are you here for this house?"

"I am."

"Who are you taking, please?"

He frowned. "The gentleman and his daughter."

"Where to?"

He rubbed his mustache. He saw my clothes, and he probably wasn't sure if he should be speaking to someone like me. "England, as far as I know. I don't take them all the way there, of course—just to the city wall. Other carriages will take them north from there."

"England?!"

"Can't blame them. The city's fighting itself and the harvests have been poor for many years. What's left?"

I stumbled back toward the iron gates. They were leaving? Was this my doing? Had my little note made Valjean decide to go away? I thought it might make them lock their doors at night or perhaps push their furniture against those doors. Or tell the police, or hide their jewels.

I didn't think they'd leave rue Plumet for good.

And why England? I knew nothing of England except that they too had a king and that it rained a lot. And it was far away.

Marius! What of him? Did he know they were going? I was sure he didn't or he'd be here too. Since Lamarque died, he'd been spending a lot of time at the Café Musain. Was he there last night? *If so, he doesn't know. He'll come here tonight and find that she's gone . . .*

I felt ill. I leaned against the railings and closed my eyes. *My vow . . . To make people happy. Marius's heart will be broken by this.*

I seized the iron bars. I wished I could climb them or be even thinner so I might slip right through. I wished . . .

And suddenly, there she was. She walked out into the morning, dressed in traveling clothes—boots and a red dress with a dark red cape. Red too was the skin near her eyes: she'd been crying. She seemed to be talking to herself.

As she came closer, I heard her: "England? Oh, God! Marius, where are you?"

I knew what to do. I breathed in, and out . . .

I stepped forward and took hold of the railings so that I stood in full view.

"Cosette?"

She'd heard me but couldn't see me. Her eyes ran the length of the railings until they found me—and she gasped.

"Cosette?" I reached out to her.

She came toward me very slowly. She looked as if she'd seen a ghost and couldn't believe it. She turned her head from left to right, as if trying to capture all sides of my face. "Eponine?"

"Yes."

"Eponine? From Montfermeil?"

"The same."

"No! How can it be?" She was very close to me now. "Is it really you? How long has it been?"

"Nine years. It'll be ten years this Christmas."

She gave a frail smile. I recognized it—the smile she'd given when she first arrived, or as we fed Gavroche. She shook her head. "I can't believe it . . . Eponine."

I flushed. "The last time you saw me I was in satin, I think. Not now . . ." I pressed my whole body against the bars, and I pressed my face between them too so that my eyes and nose and mouth fit between two bars. They would leave their mark upon my cheeks later. "Cosette . . . I'm so sorry. I'm sorry with my whole heart."

She frowned. "Sorry?"

"For every single thing that I ever did to hurt you. For all the cruelty and the mean words . . . Oh, I was horrible to you and for so long! And Cosette, I've never forgotten or forgiven myself for it. Every day, I've felt so ashamed . . ." I started to cry through the bars.

But Cosette didn't cry. In fact, her small, frail smile grew into a wider one and she murmured, "Eponine . . . Listen. I can't say they were easy days because they weren't. They were hard, and I was cold and lonely and afraid in them. I can't describe how happy I was to leave Montfermeil! I felt like I was being saved. I felt like he—dear Papa—was a miracle, in a way. But, Eponine, we were *children* . . . We didn't understand the world or know what was right and wrong."

"*I* knew! I knew that kicking you and spitting at you was wrong but I still did it . . ." I sobbed.

"But you were *told* to! I knew you were! I'd hear her—your mother—telling you to be unkind. What choice did you have?" She reached through the bars, took my hand. "You've nothing to say sorry for."

I cried even more. I'd hoped she'd curse me because I'd known curses in my life and I could bear them. But she was Cosette. She had no curses, only generosity and goodness and a beauty inside her that matched her outer kind.

No wonder he loves her.

She said, "Don't cry . . . There were times when I wished to be your friend for your sake, more than for my own. I felt so sorry for you!"

"Sorry? For me?"

"My mother was far away but at least she loved me. I'd lie on the floor at night and feel her love as if she was beside me, holding my hand." She didn't have to say anymore.

Cosette put her hand into her pocket and took out a handkerchief. It was perfectly white. "Here"—she pressed it through the railings—"no more crying. There are enough tears in the world."

"But I used to call you names! I struck you once, and—"

"You did but you were *made* to. You were never shown any other way! And anyway—those aren't the things I remember. You filled my bucket for me from the trough, remember? And we cared for the baby . . ."

"Gavroche."

"Yes, Gavroche."

I blew my nose. She watched me.

"How did you come to be like this? So thin and pale? You used to wear fur collars . . ."

I smiled through the tears. "You have those fur collars now."

She looked at me so tenderly. "What happened to you all?"

"After you left? Papa gambled all the money away. Then he killed a man—a bishop."

"Killed? Really?"

I nodded. "We ran away. For years we lived in ditches and caves, hiding from the police. Kept stealing. Came to Paris in the end. I've played my part in some awful crimes, Cosette, and I hate what I have done, but I've changed now. I made a vow last winter— to never do another bad thing in all my life." I blew my nose.

"Are you alone?"

I felt too tired to tell her much more. "Yes. Alone."

Cosette strengthened her grip on my hands. "Eponine. Let me give you some clothes, a little money."

"No, I can't take—"

"You can! We're going away and leaving lots of clothes behind us; surely you have need of them?"

"The driver of the carriage says you are going to England."

"We are. Last winter, Papa was injured by some villains and he thinks they're coming back for him." Her smile was gone now. "But, oh, it breaks my heart to go! I have no wish to leave here. My whole world is in Paris . . ."

"Because of Marius?"

She flinched. "What? You know him? How do you know him?"

"He lived where we lived, for a time. In the same building. Then I saw him in Les Jardins du Luxembourg and I knew that he loved you."

"You saw him there? And me?"

"Yes. Both reading books, or pretending to . . . I wanted to approach you, to say sorry for the things I did in Montfermeil, but I felt afraid—"

"Afraid? Of *me*?"

"I'd treated you so badly! I thought you might resent me . . ." I looked down. I could hardly bear to think of having handed Papa's letter to them—Cosette and her father. But how could I not mention it? "I did approach you, once."

"You did? I don't recall it."

"The girl with the bleeding face? A letter? She was hiding behind her hair . . ."

Cosette gasped. "That was you? You were that poor creature!"

"And the letter . . . It had lies in it. It led your father to—"

"To the Gorbeau . . ." She dropped her gaze. She did not let go of my hands but her grip loosened; I could tell she was thinking, remembering. "Papa was cut with a knife in that place . . ."

"Not by me! The knife wasn't my knife! I wasn't in that room! But, Cosette, that was the worst mistake of my life—that letter, that trick . . . I was desperate. I was a fool. I'm so sorry and I will be sorry all my life—*all* of it."

She turned back to me. Her face was calm—not a child's. She breathed out very slowly. "You've lived a very different life from mine. You've struggled to eat and stay warm, I can see that."

My voice was tiny, surprised. "You forgive me?"

She gave a small smile. "Forgiveness isn't easy—not always. But you are being honest, Eponine. And Papa survived that night, and is well—and *he'd* forgive you, I'm certain. So I shall forgive you too, poor thing. And in truth, I am scared to imagine the life you must have had, the things you've been forced to do . . ."

I began to tremble. I thought of all the bad things. "I tried to make amends, Cosette."

Her eyes were gentle. "You did? How, Eponine?"

I swallowed. "I found Marius. I led him to you."

"What?" With that, she stepped back. She put her hands to her cheeks, disbelieving.

"I heard a rumor that this house might be robbed and I'd made my vow—to be good, always—and so I came here to protect it. And I saw you . . ."

Her eyes sparkled. "Marius spoke of a girl who helped him! He told me! That was you?"

I nodded. "I wanted to help him . . . you."

"Oh!" A tear fell. "How can I ever thank you? Oh, Eponine! He's changed the world for me. How I feel is . . ."

I used a softer voice. "He doesn't know about England, does he?"

She shook her head. More tears fell so I passed the handkerchief back to her. "No. He didn't come here last night because since Lamarque's death his friends have been upset. He's been with them, trying to stop them from risking their lives . . . He promised me that he'd come to me this morning, after Lamarque's funeral procession had passed by—but I'll be gone by then! Gone! See the coach? We are leaving within minutes, Eponine! What if I never see him again? Oh, my heart! My heart breaks to think of it!"

I knew how much a heart could ache and ache. "Cosette? I will find him for you."

She looked up from the handkerchief. "You will?"

"I'm sure of it. I know where he goes—the cafés, the streets he favors. There's an old man in Austerlitz who knows him very well. Do you have an address in England? I could pass it on to him so perhaps, in time, he may join you there . . ."

Gratitude shone out of her face. "Oh, would you do that for me? Truly? Eponine, that would mean the world to me! I couldn't bear losing him! I'd never be happy again, if I did . . ."

"Of course I'll do it," I said. I owed it to them. I owed it to all the people I'd ever hurt or stolen from. I'd do it for both of them.

She ran inside and returned a moment later with a note. "Here. This is the address. You'll give it to him, Eponine? So that he may find me again?"

"I promise I will." I tucked the note inside my pocket, patted it. "It's safe in there."

We were quiet for a moment. We were both a little breathless, both so full of thoughts that words weren't enough for them. In the end, Cosette said, "We could have been good friends in Montfermeil, couldn't we? But we could be good friends now."

"Friends? You and me? But you are a beautiful lady with pearls in your ears and satin dresses . . . I sleep in a tree. I wear rags. I've got knots in my hair . . . How can we be friends?"

"Because such things don't matter! Not to me. Pearls? Satin? They're worthless in the end. It doesn't matter how much money might be in our pockets or whether we are thin or well fed: what matters is our *hearts*, and what is in them. Do you care for me?"

I nodded. "Yes, I do. You're so kind and loving."

"And I care for you. Because *you're* kind and loving, Eponine. You're honest! You've been so very honest with me . . . And you're very beautiful—inside and out. I wish you knew that you were."

I wept again. I shook my head once, as if to say, *No, no, I'm not these things*. But she grasped my wrists then.

"You *are*! How, how you are! You mustn't think that what you did nine years ago defines you, or that by giving us that letter you can't be forgiven or loved. We all make mistakes! We've all done things we wish we hadn't. But what matters is *now*, and what happens in the future. I forgive you fully for anything you ever did to me. And I would have done so even if you hadn't brought Marius to me. But you have . . . And for that, I will be indebted to you for all my life."

We held hands again. "We're friends? Despite everything?"

"Despite everything."

Then she reached through the bars and embraced me. Her arms wrapped round my shoulders and mine went forward and wrapped around hers. It was a long, tight hold. I could smell her perfume and feel her warmth. I imagined who else she had held in such a way.

I knew this: I would always feel a pain, when I thought of their love. I would always wish that he loved me instead. But her words made the pain a little less.

I sniffed, nodded. "I'll go now. I'll find him and tell him you are leaving for England and I will give him this address. You'll see him again—I know it."

"Thank you. With all my heart, thank you . . ." Then she reached into her pocket, held out her hand. "This is for you."

It was a Louis d'or. A shining star. I'd only ever seen one Louis d'or before—one Christmas Eve, inside a wooden shoe.

"It's from my father, Jean Valjean. He told me to tell you that all things can be forgiven. He said he knows who you are and what you have done, but he wishes you well, Eponine."

And then I looked up. He was standing in the highest window of the house on rue Plumet. He was looking down at us and his face was the same kind and knowing face that I'd seen in our inn so many years ago. How he'd looked at Cosette then was how he was looking at me now.

He held up a single hand, as if waving.

I took the coin. I held my hand up too, waving back.

"Go," Cosette whispered. "Find Marius."

I ran. I hurried down the rue Plumet but I paused before I turned out of sight. There she was, still watching me.

All those different kinds of love . . . My love for my siblings, my love for Marius . . . But now this love too—my love for a *friend*. That word was a new word for me. Was she a friend? Truly? I was hurting, as I ran. I would always hurt and miss him; I would always feel sad that Marius wanted *her* arms around him, not mine, and that he loved Cosette instead of loving me—and so maybe we could never be true, proper friends. But I liked that she'd believed it. I liked that she'd not minded my dark deeds, and that she'd called me beautiful. That she'd smiled and forgiven me.

She is good. She was, I knew, worthy of him.

It hurt, it hurt—but I liked the word *friend* and I ran, whispering it.

THE NOTE

They say the heart's a muscle—so can it grow stronger, over time? My arms were never very strong. The muscles inside them have always been little, as if hardly there at all, but I've seen men in the fields—plowing or bringing in the hay—whose arms were so big they could lift the big bales straight into the air and carry them over their heads. With hard work, muscles grow stronger.

My heart loved my family and bits of Montfermeil. But then I met Marius—and my heart loved him so much that I think it actually became a bigger heart, and it loved so many more things.

I loved Cosette's note in my pocket, the sound of my feet as I ran. I loved the evening sky and my breathing and the word *friend* and I loved the silhouette of Montmartre's hill and the Louis d'or, which I'd tucked into my underclothes so I wouldn't lose it. I loved the way that Jean Valjean had waved at me from the window, and I'd waved back.

This was a hard world, I knew that. It was dangerous; it had its knives and lies and cruelties, and Paris felt on the edge of such trouble. But there were small wonders too—everywhere. And I loved that I was living when so many others weren't.

Find Marius! Give him this note.

I had a future. Suddenly, I saw that—a future! Had I really had one before? I had never thought about the days to come. I was poor, so I thought of each meal and where I might spend the night and no further. But a Louis d'or? And forgiveness?

Everything was possible now.

Find him. Find the funeral procession of Lamarque. That was where he'd be. I ran fast, but the day was so hot that I paused in the shade of Les Jardins du Luxembourg to catch my breath and wipe my brow. I could feel the sweat from my body soaking into my dress and the cloth was damp to the touch. *What about the note? What if my sweat makes the ink run, and the note can't be read at all?* All would be lost, and useless. So I sat on a bench (*his* bench) and, taking a deep breath, I read the note myself:

My dearest Marius,

Papa has insisted that we leave Paris today—him and I. He fears for our safety. I don't want to go! How can I leave when we've just found each other and you're here? I can't bear it. I just want to be where you are.

Below, I've written the address that we're heading for. It's in the north of Paris—we're staying there for a few weeks until Papa can secure our passage by sea to England. Marius, could you live an English life?

The good and gentle Eponine is bringing this note to you. We owe our happiness to her, sweet thing.

Stay safe and be careful—and remember that I love you, I love you, and I will never stop.

Find me, Marius? I'll pray that you do.

Your loving Cosette x

I touched the word *love* wherever it was written down. Then I took my finger to my written name, those seven letters: *Eponine* . . . I'd never seen it written in such a dainty hand.

The good and gentle Eponine. Sweet thing.

I folded the letter and tucked it away. He'd be following the coffin of his hero, walking very solemnly with his hand across his heart and saying good-bye to the man he'd called *our only hope.* He'd be saying good-bye to his younger self too, maybe, because he was in love now—and it was Cosette he'd follow, for always.

Find him. Promise me?

I pocketed the note and ran on and on.

I'd never seen the streets like this. There was shouting and screaming and crying out. Stones were thrown and men were fighting—fists were smashing into cheekbones and jawbones and bellies and ribs. I winced. It made me think of Babet because he could make a fist. Montparnasse too.

Houses were on fire. The streets were filled with black smoke so that I couldn't see clearly. I grabbed the wrist of a man. "Monsieur?"

His face was bloody. "What?"

"What's happening here? Why is Paris on fire and so angry?" It was meant to be a mournful day.

"The funeral procession? People climbed onto the carriage and shouted for freedom, and *Vive la république!* And soldiers opened fire on it and killed some, and now everyone is fighting. Now is the time!"

"Now?"

"To change France, and free it! Just as Lamarque wanted to!"

People were killed?

He turned and said, "Keep away from here—understand me? It's no place for women. This is man's work and more men will die before the day is over. Find safety, do you hear?"

He ran down the smoky street.

But I'd never been safe in all my life and wouldn't look for it now. All that mattered was finding Marius.

A GIRL AS A BOY

I hurried on and didn't care for the shouting and rage, or the smoke.

Take them all down!

Down with the king! Fight for Lamarque!

I ran down alleyways where the sun never reached. I needed to get to rue de la Chanvrerie and the place Saint-Michel and the Café Musain because that's where he'd be, now. *If he's still alive*—and my heart clenched with fear at that thought.

There was a clattering then and out of the smoke came a loose, white horse, snorting as it went. It seemed so strange—so ghostly and white. Where was its rider? What was it fleeing from?

Soon I saw. There was a barricade at the end of the street. A smell of sewers and gunpowder hung in the air. The barricade was made of chairs and barrels and desks and wardrobes and carts and tables, piled high to make a huge wall. I'd never seen anything like it. I'd heard tales of barricades but I didn't know they'd be so big that I could hardly see the top of them.

"You there!" I was seized. It was a young man I didn't recognize. He smelled of his own sweat and his hair stuck to his forehead and he said, "This isn't a place for women! Are you crazy? Go!"

"I'm looking for a man—"

"I don't care! You won't find him! He'll be either fighting or dead and he won't want to see you! And what good's a woman to us? We need fighters, not a scruffy girl who's far too thin to fight . . . Get away!" He pushed me.

I stumbled back. "But I have a note for him!"

"You're a nuisance! Go, or I will . . ." He raised his fist.

I ran back into the shadows. How could I get to the rue de la Chanvrerie? Or even get through the barricades and crowds of men?

It was true: there weren't any women anywhere. They were all inside, I supposed—hiding, like I should be.

I felt Cosette's note pressed against me. *What good's a woman to us?*

So I thought: *I'll dress like a boy.*

That was the way. I'd dress as a boy and run through the barricades shouting, *"Vive la France!"* and no one would stop me. They'd think, *He's just one of us.*

But how could I find boys' clothes? I'd seen them on washing lines, strung out from house to house, but I couldn't take them. To take them would be stealing, and I'd promised not to steal again.

I'd have to find another way. In my left pocket, I felt the Louis d'or.

I could buy boys' clothes. To buy clothes! Had I ever? But now, I had money and I could buy clothes like normal people did! *Yes. I'll do that.*

I ran from street to street. Whenever I found a tailor's shop I knocked on the door and called, "Let me in! I need clothes! Breeches and a shirt—and I can pay you well!" But all the shops were shut.

What now?

I closed my eyes very tightly. *Think, Eponine . . .* My belly growled with hunger.

Hunger. I thought of chestnuts.

The chestnut-seller! I opened my eyes. Him! Hadn't he been kind to me and spoken of a son who was my age? I remembered him saying, *We must help, when we can.*

He had stood on the corner of rue de Pontoise and the passage des Patriarches. It wasn't so far away.

I fled there, away from the barricades so that the gunshots grew quieter as I made my way. What if he wasn't there? It wasn't chestnut season.

But he was there. He was standing exactly where I'd hoped he might be and instead of chestnuts, he was boiling eggs in a metal pail. He was sunburnt and looked older. *Who wants eggs? On a day of such fighting?*

"Monsieur? Do you remember me?"

He looked up. He seemed very sad and I thought, *He mourns Lamarque.*

"We met last winter. You were roasting chestnuts and I asked for a single one because I was so cold and hungry and you gave me a handful. Remember?"

I saw in his eyes that yes, he remembered. "You don't look much better, Mademoiselle. Still too thin."

"I know. But, Monsieur, it isn't food I'm looking for. I need help." At that moment, I showed him my Louis d'or.

He stepped back, gasped. Then he hurriedly looked about him, said, "Hide that! That is a goodly amount of money and you could be robbed. These are dark times . . ."

"I want to give it to you in return for some boys' clothing."

He frowned. "Boys' clothing. You'd pay me a whole Louis d'or for boys' clothing? What on earth for?"

"I've got to get through the barricades and they won't let women through."

"So . . . you want to dress like a boy?"

"Yes."

"Mademoiselle . . ." He shook his head very vigorously. "No, no. It's not safe! You heard of what happened? At Lamarque's funeral procession? There are hundreds dead already and the fires will burn long into the night . . ."

"I know, but I have to find someone. It's very, very important that I give him a note. You've got a son?"

"I do. But his clothes aren't worth a whole Louis d'or."

"They would be to me."

"It'd be far too much money and I couldn't accept . . ."

"I'd give the coin freely. Think of it as a thank-you—for your kindness in the winter, which meant so much to me."

He looked at the coin. I knew it was more money than chestnuts or eggs could ever give him. "So be it," he said. "I'll help you. What do you need? A chemise? Breeches?"

"And a cap to hide my hair."

"Boots?" He saw my feet.

"I've been barefoot for years, Monsieur. Let your son keep his boots."

"I live nearby," he said. "If you wait here, I will get them."

I nodded and waited. When he returned he carried a simple flannelette shirt and brown woolen trousers. The trousers were too large so I had to tighten them with string and roll their bottoms up. A leather cap hid my hair. I kept Cosette's note tucked in my underclothes.

As for my ragged dress, I offered it to him.

"No," he said. "Take it. You may have need of it—as bandages, perhaps."

I pressed the Louis d'or into his palm. I closed his fingers around it and hoped it would bring him happiness and safety, and a better life.

"Be careful." He looked tender, almost fatherly. I thanked him, and ran—a girl dressed as a boy—into the gloom of night.

THE BARRICADE

No skirts and no swinging hair. Eponine the boy. I ran back to the rue de la Chanvrerie, afraid of nothing. I just thought, *Him . . . him . . .* as I leapt over a pothole.

The breeches and the leather cap meant that no one noticed me. No hand reached out to grasp me and no one called out, *This isn't a place for you!* I ran past other boys and they were all dirty-faced and wide-eyed and maybe they heard my footsteps and thought I was a soldier with a musket or a revolutionary like them or just a young urchin—I didn't care. I was alive and running. Helping two people.

I ran over the river. There were bodies in it, floating among the weeds.

On, on to the Café Musain. I took side streets and alleyways because I knew that soldiers would be marching in the boulevards. Everything looked different. There weren't any carts or barrows anymore; all movable things were gone, even doors. There was blood underfoot.

A body. I saw it slumped against a wall. I stumbled, pressed my hands to my mouth, scared it might be him. His eyes were open. His chest was open too—like a red, wet cave.

I retched.

It's not Marius. I exhaled with relief—but I was frightened now. Suddenly I understood the darkness around me and I trembled as I turned on to the rue de la Chanvrerie. I wanted to see the Café Musain as it had always been—lively, warm, and candlelit. But it didn't look like that now.

Where the café had been, there was a barricade.

It was huge, far bigger than the other one, towering above me like a cathedral and reaching up toward the sky. Chairs and tables and barrels and doors and wagons and cartwheels and wardrobes and desks and what seemed to be the frame of a bed all glowered down on me. Even so, how could this protect them? I'd seen what a musket ball could do and if it could break through the bones of a poor man's chest it could splinter a wardrobe or break a chair.

"Halt! Stand there!"

The voice was very angry.

"You, boy! What do you want?"

Boy? I thought he was speaking to someone else. Then I remembered.

I looked up. On the uppermost part of the barricade stood a man I recognized. It was Enjolras—the boy with curly blond hair. He pointed. "You! Speak!"

I couldn't say, *Don't you remember me?* Because I wasn't a girl anymore. So I cried, "I've come to join the barricades!"

He paused. "You're for a republic? You'd see the monarchy defeated?"

I shook a little. In the deepest voice I could manage I said, "Yes, I would."

"How old are you, boy?"

"Seventeen. Old enough!"

"And your name?"

What name could I give? Both Thenardier and Jondrette were hateful, thieving names. What was left? "Just Boy!"

"Boy? *Garçon?* That's your name?"

"It's the name I go by. What does a name matter? What matters is France, Monsieur! *Vive la république!*"

He stared from his wooden tower. Perhaps he thought he knew me or had seen a girl with a face a bit like this boy's but he didn't say so. "Do you have weapons, Boy?"

"No weapons."

"Never mind. We have ones to spare. Walk to your right, toward the lantern, and we'll help you through." He seemed to step back but then he suddenly called out again as if checking for the final time, "You'd be willing to die for the cause? It may come to that."

I knew the answer. Willing to die for the republic, and for France? No, I wasn't prepared to do that because that wasn't my cause or what I dreamed of. But to die for my own cause? For the sake of the man I loved and for his own happiness? For the sake of a little goodness, in a dark world?

"Yes!"

He nodded. "To the right. I'll come down."

* * *

He had the gray shadows of sleeplessness and worry beneath his eyes, as if someone had smeared ink there with their thumb.

"Come in."

I ducked under. I was behind the barricades.

I looked around. I saw the street I'd known before the barricades had been built around it—the stunted tree and the cobbled ground. The small butcher's shop was empty and the deep drain in front of it had been blocked with wet straw to stop soldiers creeping up through it. I'd seen dogs waiting by this butcher's shop, tongues lolling. It seemed a long time ago.

And there it was—the Café Musain. It was in the heart of it all, as if the barricade had grown from the café itself like a mushroom from soil. There were no songs here now. A small fire burned and men and boys sat around it—warming their hands. I recognized the boy with half-moon spectacles. Pistols and rifles lay against the bar's wall. I was glad to be dressed as a boy with my hair tucked under my cap.

Marius wasn't here.

"I'm Enjolras. The barricade is newly made—but hourly more and more come to join us, just like you've done. We grow stronger in number. We've got a runner too—a boy younger than yourself—who tells us that we outnumber the soldiers who have gathered on rue de Vertbois, three streets away. They'll attack soon—tonight, perhaps—but we're ready for them." He looked at me. "You can shoot a gun?"

"No," I confessed. "I never have."

"No matter. It's easy and you can learn. Or perhaps you could be a runner too—alongside Gavroche."

"Gavroche?"

"Our boy. The urchin."

"He's called Gavroche?"

"He is."

"He's ten years old, perhaps? No older?"

Enjolras frowned. "You know him?"

I caught myself. "I know his sister, I think. He's well?"

"Quite well." He smiled a little. "He's spirited, isn't he? Determined. He's never afraid and he's singing all the time . . ."

I smiled back. I didn't think my heart could be any fuller with love, but now it was. My little man—as warm as baked bread, as curious as an explorer setting out in the world. Eyes bright like the moon. Gavroche.

I reached for Enjolras. "Will you take care of him?"

He half laughed. "What? Of course—or I'll do my best to."

"His sister would be grateful. She loves him very much."

If the shadow of a thought passed through his mind, his face didn't show it. He only touched me on the shoulder and then he walked away.

Other men—young and old, wounded and healthy—came to the barricades too. Enjolras pressed guns into their hands. He showed them the fire and told them to warm themselves, or eat. There wasn't much talking. Only the scrape of a spoon against a bowl, or a whispered voice.

By the fire's light, I searched for Marius but didn't find him. *He must be here*, I thought. But where?

I looked up at the stars. Did they recognize me, in my boys' clothes? They did. I imagined them saying, *We can see you, Eponine.*

Enjolras climbed to the top of the barricades and nestled into them. I saw his silhouette against the stars and knew he was on guard, looking out. A night breeze moved his curls. I might have thought him handsome if I didn't love Marius so much.

I climbed up carefully—from chair to wagon, from barrel to chair. "Enjolras?"

He was looking out across the rooftops of Paris. "Isn't it beautiful? When it's like this, it's hard to imagine the suffering this city has seen, to believe that people are starving."

It did look very beautiful. Even where smoke rose up or where we could see another barricade. Gunfire crackled.

"Do you know a man called Marius?"

"Marius?" With that, he turned. "I do. Why do you ask?"

"He's a friend of mine. I thought he might be here so I could fight beside him."

He nodded. "You could, if he wasn't so . . ."

I waited for the word.

". . . lost."

"Lost?"

He shook his head. "He was here earlier. He was at the funeral procession with us but then he broke away, saying he couldn't be away from the girl he loved. He left. Who knows where he is now? He isn't here, anyway."

I stared. I couldn't believe it. He wasn't here? I'd dressed as a boy and run down through the bleeding, burning streets for no reason at all? "Not *here*?"

"He went to her—Colette? A name like that. It must be a love I've no knowledge of because I can't think that any love would take *me* away from *this*, our cause." He seemed disappointed. "He should be here, Boy. He should be fighting at his friends' sides."

"But love," I whispered, "can be so very strong."

"So it seems."

I looked at the rooftops. I tried to think. What must have happened? He'd have left the funeral procession and run to the rue Plumet. But he'd have found the house empty. He'd have found Cosette gone with no word or reason—and so where was he now? Wandering Paris with a broken heart?

I felt tearful. *I'll never find him now*—not in a city of ruins and fire.

The Quiet Hours

I climbed down. I found a corner near the Café Musain and nestled into it.

I didn't sleep. Others tried to—they lay down on the ground or against the barricade itself. Some talked very softly. Inside the café, I could see a man was cleaning the rifles and I wondered if he was a husband or father.

The stars above. What could they see? A Paris on fire. A fighting world. They could see Marius, wherever he was.

Keep him safe. And her.

Perhaps I slept a little because after a while, the men's soft murmuring sounded like water. I dreamed of an upturned boat and of my mother. I saw a snowy morning in Montfermeil where every single fence post wore its own hat of snow.

I dreamed of Gavroche too. I could hear his voice and he was saying, *They're coming, Enjolras! They're coming!* And I stirred then because why was Enjolras in a snowy Montfermeil?

I opened my eyes. Gavroche was standing there, puffing hard. His hair was long and he was taller, but it was still him.

"The soldiers are coming, everyone! I've seen them! They're standing up and getting ready and they'll be here soon!"

The men jumped up and drew their pistols or ran to get their rifles. "To your posts!" called Enjolras—and there was a rush of feet and hands and voices. I wanted to go to Gavroche and take off my cap and say, *Look. It's me—Eponine* . . . But I couldn't. All I could think was, *Be safe, be safe, my darling brother who deserved so much better than a life like this.*

He ducked between two chairs and was gone from sight.

A Hole in the Heart and Hand

I had heard gunfire—a crack! A snap! I knew its sound but I'd never *felt* gunfire before. When it happens near you, it booms so that your heart and lungs seem to shudder under your skin, and you stumble.

I fell. There was dust everywhere. I couldn't see for the powdery air and I couldn't stop coughing. Something heavy was crushing me—chairs and desks?—and with a second gunshot more wood came down on me like splintery rain.

There was a warm wetness on my face, trickling down from my hairline.

A third shot. More dust and more shouting and I heard Enjolras scream, "Fire back! Fire back!" and there was a thundering of musket fire that shook the ground.

I managed to crawl free. I licked my lips and tasted blood.

Get up! I managed it—but then a fifth gunshot tore into the barricades. Suddenly there was a hole in the middle of it, smoky and black, and I saw soldiers through it. They wore red coats with shining buttons and high leather boots. They knelt, lifted their rifles, and aimed.

"Fire! Fire!"

Another shot and another and another, and the windows of the Café Musain shattered, spraying glass. People were screaming "Over here!" or "Coufreyac is hit!" or "My eyes! I can't see!" or "Grantaire is dead!" or "Lord, save us!" and Enjolras was shouting, "Hold strong, have faith! *Vive la France!*" But the soldiers didn't stop. A shot passed so close to me that I fell and landed on my side, onto broken glass.

As I lay, I reached beneath my clothes: The note was still there. Then I heard him.

Marius. It was his voice! I knew it! There was so much noise around me but I heard his voice and I clambered to my feet. I shouted, "Marius!" and lunged through the smoke with my arms stretched out. Marius, who I loved more than anything, even if he didn't love me. I called his name again and again.

There. His face was smeared with dirt and his clothes were torn but it was still him. He reached for his gun, lifted it.

He thinks she's gone forever. I knew a broken heart when I saw it.

I began to stumble toward him but then a dark-eyed man grabbed me, saying, "Get yourself a gun, Boy! The wall's been breached—can't you see? They'll kill us all!" But I didn't listen, I didn't care, I just wanted to get to Marius and so I pushed the man aside. But Marius had vanished! In those few seconds! Where to? I stepped over bodies, searched the Café Musain and the shadows but I couldn't see him.

The barricade was burning. I had to raise my hand to protect my face from its heat and brightness, and I pleaded with the fire: *Please let me find him.*

Suddenly he was standing next to me. He was shielding his face too and he shouted, "She's gone!" I followed his gaze.

Enjolras shouted back, "Gone?"

"Left! Without a word! What do I have to live for now, Enjolras? So yes, I'm back! I'll fight to the death beside my friends!"

If I'd loved him before, it was nothing compared to now.

He couldn't die—never. He had to read this letter, have this letter pressed into his hand so he'd know that Cosette still loved him, so he'd know life was worth living and that he mustn't die tonight, on these barricades.

"Marius!"

But he didn't hear me. And at that very moment I saw a red-coated soldier kneeling, beyond the flames. He was narrowing an eye. He was taking aim. His rifle was aimed at Marius. All I thought was, *Not him.*

It was all I'd ever wanted—*love.* More than food or shelter, or a warm bed. I felt it, for him.

And that was what made me run toward the soldier. I ran through the smoke, through the heat of burning wood . . . ten, eleven, twelve steps that felt like forever . . . *Not him, not him.* The soldier didn't see me—his eyes were on his target—so I threw my right hand across the end of the musket and pulled it toward myself.

I felt nothing as I fell. Just love, which rushed out of me, as warm and red as blood.

Rue de la Chanvrerie,
June 5, 1832

So here I am. All these things and words and moments have led me to this. To lying here.

The street's quiet now.

The musket fire has stopped. There's a soft peace around me so all I can hear is my own ragged breath—and hooves? Yes, the horse is still near me. It's pulling a cart that's taking the bodies away.

Most of the young men are dead. I saw them fall as I fell. Since I've been lying here, I've heard them cry for help. Someone was praying near me but he's stopped now.

Enjolras is dead. All his friends are.

But not Marius. Marius isn't dead because I put my hand across that musket and afterward I heard him shouting, *"Retreat! Retreat! Find safety, for God's sake!"* So I know he's alive.

The clock chimes. *One, two, three* . . . I wait and count. It's midnight now.

* * *

Can't move. Can't swallow. Can't breathe.

I'll die. But Gavroche will keep singing his songs. Papa will keep stealing. One day I think Azelma will stop because her heart's a good heart, deep down. The man called Valjean? He'll head north with his sun-haired daughter, stand on a blowing beach and look at the English sea. Cosette will weep, thinking, *I don't want to leave him, I don't want to leave him* . . .

I don't want to leave him either.

The note. I still have it. I promised Cosette I'd give Marius the note but I've failed.

Those stars. There'll always be twinkling eyes in the night sky. It's hard to imagine it—fifty years from now. Or one hundred. Or two hundred. What will the world be like? I don't know. But I know the starry sky will look the same.

Bring him to me, stars. I have this letter. I made a promise.

I see his face. I see him perfectly—his brown eyes, his dimples, his mouth. His face blocks the stars.

"Are you alive? Boy? Isn't that your name? Talk to me."

It's a strange dream. He is calling me Boy—why Boy? I'm Eponine.

He is so close. He's kneeling so that I feel his breath on me and it's not a dream at all. I'm awake and he's here.

"Marius?" I can only whisper.

He frowns. "You know my name?"

"Yes. You don't"—I try to swallow—"recognize me?"

He stares. "I don't."

"It's Eponine. Remember? I—"

His face changes. It softens and opens up and he says, "Eponine? What the . . . ? Why are you here? And dressed as a boy?"

"Girls aren't allowed"—I try to smile—"on the barricades. But I'm . . . dying. See?"

He looks where he's kneeling and sees my blood. "Oh . . . you're very badly wounded . . . but listen to me: I'll carry you to the Café Musain, where there are a few others who survived, and who could mend—"

"The soldiers?"

"They've gone. It's safe now. I'll carry you . . ."

He takes hold of my hand.

I scream. It's shrill and sudden, bursting out of me because the pain is too much, too much.

"I hurt you? But I only touched your hand!"

"Look . . . My hand's gone. The musket . . . I held the end . . ."

"You held the end of a musket? *Why?*"

"Because it was being aimed."

"Aimed?"

"At you."

He pales. "Me?"

"You were standing. There were flames. A soldier saw you and knelt . . . aimed . . ."

"The boy. I saw a boy fall . . . That was you?"

"Yes."

Marius makes a sound. It's like a far smaller bullet has hit him. "Eponine . . . You silly thing . . . Why did you do that? Why did you get in the way of the gun? Still, they'll mend you because a missing hand won't kill you, not if we stop this blood and—"

"Marius. There's more, I'm sure. My body hurts. The side of me . . ."

He looks again. Then he drops his gaze. *"Mon Dieu . . ."* He knows: There's not enough blood inside me anymore. Not enough beats left in my heart.

"I asked the stars and they brought you here."

"What?" He comes nearer.

I can hardly hear my own voice now. "May I ask something of you?"

"Oui, Eponine."

"Stay with me? I don't want to die alone. Stay by my side?"

He sits down. Very carefully, he moves his arm beneath me so he's half holding me. "Of course. I'm here." His eyes look so sad. "Many have died tonight—good souls—but I'm still living, Eponine. Why?"

"It's right that you are."

"Is it? You shouldn't have grabbed that musket . . . I've got nothing to live for. The woman I love's gone . . ."

"No," I whisper. "Come nearer . . ."

He bends down.

"I've got a note."

"A note?"

"From her."

"Cosette?" He tenses. "How? I left the funeral procession to be with her but she was gone—without a word! After all our promises . . ."

"I saw her . . . She wrote a note and asked me to deliver it to you so you'd know—" I cry out in pain.

"Oh! Oh!" He lifts my head a little, puts something soft beneath it. "Does that help?"

"A little." I can see him better now. I could just look at his face for the rest of my life, but I've got to keep talking. I say it quickly, in one breath: "She asked me to give you this note so you know she loves you. She doesn't want to leave. It has"—I shudder—"her address so you might find her. Be with her."

He smiles, but there are tears in his eyes. "A note? Where is it?"

"Safe . . . in my waistband . . ."

He looks down. "May I . . . ?"

"It hurts so much . . ."

"I know . . ." He's so careful as he unties the string around my waist that I barely feel him. I close my eyes. *He is touching me.*

"I have it," he says, and his face is lit like a hundred thousand stars.

"Marius? Before you read it?"

He looks down at me. I've got seconds left, no more. I know that. "Kiss me?" He says nothing, but I see that familiar crease appear between his eyes. "Not on my lips and not when I'm living because that would be untrue and unfair. But on my forehead? When I'm dead?" I hear myself sob. "As a friend?"

He nods.

"You'll stay with me?"

"I'll stay. You won't be alone."

"And a kiss?"

"I promise. When you've closed your eyes."

* * *

He's holding me. He's looking at me.

My love. My love. I've seen him in every season. I walked with him on a warm summer's evening . . . He made my world feel new.

What else? I see the sunlight on the Seine, and Cosette's hands holding on to mine. I hear the gray nag's whicker as I rub her nose, and I feel Gavroche sucking milk from my fingers. Warm fruit. A breeze, high up.

How lucky I've been.

And I've seen him take her note. He'll find her now. Marius will find Cosette and they'll marry and have children and perhaps on winter nights they'll sit with their children and tell them the story of a girl they once knew called Eponine who brought them together.

I open my eyes.

He's watching me. His smile is soft. He strokes my hair and I feel a peace that I've never known—here, in his arms.

Very quietly, I say, "You know . . . Monsieur Marius?"

He smiles. "Mademoiselle Eponine?"

"I think I was a little in love with you."

His eyes shine and I can see my reflection in them. But I like the girl I see. She looks happy. Why, I wonder, when she is dying? Perhaps it's because she knows Marius does love her, in his way. He will not forget her.

I smile. I'm not alone—Marius is with me. I'm not afraid anymore.

We all leave something behind us. A bird in flight will lose a snow-white feather, and flowers in the hedgerows will drop their petals. And people? We leave memories. Footprints in the dust and fingerprints on everything we've touched, warmth in every hand we've held. We become stories that are spoken of, for always. And in this way, we carry on.

I feel his lips. They are on my forehead—warm, warm—as he lays me down. "Oh, Eponine . . ."

And now my love's shining out of me, filling the streets and fields and sky, and all I can think is, *He lives, he lives.* And perhaps I live too and always will, for love is the strongest thing of all—and love never dies, never dies.

ACKNOWLEDGMENTS

This book has been both a delight and a privilege. I am grateful to everyone at Chicken House for their warmth, knowledge, and care—but particular thanks to Barry Cunningham and my wonderful editor, Rachel Leyshon; I've loved working with you all. My thanks, too, to my family, whose support is the foundation of every book. And lastly, I am grateful—as always—to my agent, Vivienne Schuster, who is to me as the stars are to Eponine—wise, reassuring, and always there.

ABOUT THE AUTHOR

Susan E. Fletcher is the author of several books for adults, including *Eve Green*, which won a Whitbread First Novel Award in the United Kingdom. *A Little in Love* is her first book for young adults. Susan lives in England. You can follow her on Twitter at @sfletcherauthor.